The Library of Babel

T0332982

Jorge Luis Borges

The Library of Babel

Translated by
Andrew Hurley

PENGUIN CLASSICS
an imprint of
PENGUIN BOOKS

PENGUIN CLASSICS

UK | USA | Canada | Ireland | Australia
India | New Zealand | South Africa

Penguin Books is part of the Penguin Random House group of companies
whose addresses can be found at global.penguinrandomhouse.com.

Penguin
Random House
UK

These translations first published in *Collected Fictions* in the USA by
Viking Penguin, a member of Penguin Putnam Inc. 1998
Published in Penguin Books, 2000
Selected from *Fictions* Penguin Classics 2000 and *The Book of Sand and
Shakespeare's Memory* Penguin Classics 2001
This selection published in Little Clothbound Classics 2023
003

Cover design and illustration by Coralie Bickford-Smith

Copyright © María Kodama, 1998
Translation copyright © Penguin Putnam Inc., 1998

Set in 10/14.5pt Baskerville 10 Pro
Typeset by Jouve (UK), Milton Keynes
Printed and bound in Great Britain by Clays Ltd, Elcograf S.p.A.

The authorized representative in the EEA is Penguin Random House Ireland,
Morrison Chambers, 32 Nassau Street, Dublin D02 YH68

A CIP catalogue record for this book is available from the British Library

ISBN: 978–0–241–63086–0

Contents

The Garden of Forking Paths

For Victoria Ocampo

On page 242 of *The History of the World War,* Liddell Hart tells us that an Allied offensive against the Serre-Montauban line (to be mounted by thirteen British divisions backed by one thousand four hundred artillery pieces) had been planned for July 24, 1916, but had to be put off until the morning of the twenty-ninth. Torrential rains (notes Capt. Liddell Hart) were the cause of that delay – a delay that entailed no great consequences, as it turns out. The statement which follows – dictated, reread, and signed by Dr Yu Tsun, former professor of English in the *Hochschule* at Tsingtao – throws unexpected light on the case. The two first pages of the statement are missing.

*

. . . and I hung up the receiver. Immediately afterward, I recognised the voice that had answered in German. It was that of Capt. Richard Madden. Madden's presence in Viktor Runeberg's flat meant the end of our efforts and (though this seemed to me quite secondary, or *should have seemed*) our lives as well. It meant that Runeberg had been arrested, or murdered.* Before the sun set on that day, I would face the same fate. Madden was implacable – or rather, he was obliged to be implacable. An Irishman at the orders of the English, a man accused of a certain lack of zealousness, perhaps even treason, how could he fail to embrace and give thanks for this miraculous favour – the discovery, capture, perhaps death, of two agents of the German Empire? I went upstairs to my room; absurdly, I locked the door, and then I threw myself, on my back, onto my narrow iron bed. Outside the window were the usual rooftops and the overcast six o'clock sun. I found it incredible that this

---

* A bizarre and despicable supposition. The Prussian spy Hans Rabener, alias Viktor Runeberg, had turned an automatic pistol on his arresting officer, Capt. Richard Madden. Madden, in self-defense, inflicted the wounds on Rabener that caused his subsequent death. [Ed. note.]

day, lacking all omens and premonitions, should be the day of my implacable death. Despite my deceased father, despite my having been a child in a symmetrical garden in Hai Feng – was I, now, about to die? Then I reflected that all things happen to *oneself,* and happen precisely, precisely *now.* Century follows century, yet events occur only *in the present;* countless men in the air, on the land and sea, yet everything that truly happens, happens *to me* . . . The almost unbearable memory of Madden's horsey face demolished those mental ramblings. In the midst of my hatred and my terror (now I don't mind talking about terror – now that I have foiled Richard Madden, now that my neck hungers for the rope), it occurred to me that that brawling and undoubtedly happy warrior did not suspect that I possessed the Secret – the name of the exact location of the new British artillery park on the Ancre. A bird furrowed the grey sky, and I blindly translated it into an aeroplane, and that aeroplane into many (in the French sky), annihilating the artillery park with vertical bombs. If only my throat, before a bullet crushed it, could cry out that name so that it might be heard in Germany . . . But my human voice was so terribly inadequate. How was I to make it reach the Leader's ear – the ear of that sick and hateful man who knew nothing of Runeberg and me save that we were in Staffordshire, and who was vainly awaiting word from us in his arid office in Berlin, poring infinitely through the newspapers? . . . *I must flee,* I said aloud. I sat up noiselessly, in needless but perfect silence, as though Madden were already just outside my door. Something – perhaps the mere show of proving that my resources were nonexistent – made me go through my pockets. I found what I knew I would find: the American watch, the nickel-plated chain and quadrangular coin, the key ring with the compromising and useless keys to Runeberg's flat, the notebook, a letter I resolved to destroy at once (and never did), the false passport, one crown, two shillings, and a few odd pence, the red-and-blue pencil, the handkerchief, the revolver with its single bullet. Absurdly, I picked it up and hefted it, to give myself courage. I vaguely reflected that a pistol shot can be heard at a considerable distance. In ten minutes, my plan was ripe. The telephone book gave me the name of the only person able to communicate the information: he lived in a suburb of Fenton, less than a half hour away by train.

I am a coward. I can say that, now that I have carried out a plan whose dangerousness and daring no man will deny. I know that it was a terrible thing to do. I did not do it for Germany. What do I care for a barbaric country that has forced me to the ignominy of spying? Furthermore, I know of a man of England – a modest man – who in my view is no less a genius than Goethe. I spoke with him for no more than an hour, but for one hour he was Goethe ... No – I did it because I sensed that the Leader looked down on the people of my race – the countless ancestors whose blood flows through my veins. I wanted to prove to him that a yellow man could save his armies. And I had to escape from Madden. His hands, his voice, could beat upon my door at any moment. I silently dressed, said goodbye to myself in the mirror, made my way downstairs, looked up and down the quiet street, and set off. The train station was not far from my flat, but I thought it better to take a cab. I argued that I ran less chance of being recognized that way; the fact is, I felt I was visible and vulnerable – infinitely vulnerable – in the deserted street. I recall that I told the driver to stop a little distance from the main entrance to the station. I got down from the cab with willed and almost painful slowness. I would be going to the village of Ashgrove, but I bought a ticket for a station farther down the line. The train was to leave at eight-fifty, scant minutes away. I had to hurry; the next train would not be until nine-thirty. There was almost no one on the platform. I walked through the cars; I recall a few workmen, a woman dressed in mourning weeds, a young man fervently reading Tacitus' *Annals,* and a cheerful-looking wounded soldier. The train pulled out at last. A man I recognised ran, vainly, out to the end of the platform; it was Capt. Richard Madden. Shattered, trembling, I huddled on the other end of the seat, far from the feared window.

From that shattered state I passed into a state of almost abject cheerfulness. I told myself that my duel had begun, and that in dodging my adversary's thrust – even by forty minutes, even thanks to the slightest smile from fate – the first round had gone to me. I argued that this small win prefigured total victory. I argued that the win was not really even so small, since without the precious hour that the trains had given me, I'd be in gaol, or dead. I argued (no less sophistically) that my cowardly cheerfulness proved that I was a man capable of following this adventure through to its successful end. From that weakness I drew strength that was never to abandon me. I foresee that mankind will resign itself more and more fully every day to more and more horrendous undertakings; soon there will be nothing but warriors and brigands. I give them this piece of advice: *He who is to perform a horrendous act should imagine to himself that it is already done, should impose upon himself a future as irrevocable as the past.* That is what I did, while my eyes – the eyes of a man already dead – registered the flow of that day perhaps to be my last, and the spreading of the night. The train ran sweetly, gently, through woods of ash trees. It stopped virtually in the middle of the countryside. No one called out the name of the station. 'Ashgrove?' I asked some boys on the platform. 'Ashgrove,' they said, nodding. I got off the train.

A lamp illuminated the platform, but the boys' faces remained within the area of shadow. 'Are you going to Dr Stephen Albert's house?' one queried. Without waiting for an answer, another of them said: 'The house is a far way, but you'll not get lost if you follow that road there to the left, and turn left at every crossing.' I tossed them a coin (my last), went down some stone steps, and started down the solitary road. It ran ever so slightly downhill and was of elemental dirt. Branches tangled overhead, and the low round moon seemed to walk along beside me.

For one instant, I feared that Richard Madden had somehow seen through my desperate plan, but I soon realized that that was impossible. The boy's advice to turn always to the left reminded me that that was the common way of discovering the central lawn of a certain type of maze. I am something of a *connoisseur* of mazes: not for nothing am I the great-grandson of that Ts'ui Pen who was governor of Yunan province and who renounced all temporal power in order to write a novel containing more characters than the *Hung Lu Meng* and construct a labyrinth in which all men would lose their way. Ts'ui Pen devoted thirteen years to those disparate labours, but the hand of a foreigner murdered him and his novel made no sense and no one ever found the labyrinth. It was under English trees that I meditated on that lost labyrinth: I pictured it perfect and inviolate on the secret summit of a mountain; I pictured its outlines blurred by rice paddies, or underwater; I pictured it as infinite – a labyrinth not of octagonal pavillions and paths that turn back upon themselves, but of rivers and provinces and kingdoms ... I imagined a labyrinth of labyrinths, a maze of mazes, a twisting, turning, ever-widening labyrinth that contained both past and future and somehow implied the stars. Absorbed in those illusory imaginings, I forgot that I was a pursued man; I felt myself, for an indefinite while, the abstract perceiver of the world. The vague, living countryside, the moon, the remains of the day did their work in me; so did the gently downward road, which forestalled all possibility of weariness. The evening was near, yet infinite.

The road dropped and forked as it cut through the now-formless meadows. A keen and vaguely syllabic song, blurred by leaves and distance, came and went on the gentle gusts of breeze. I was struck by the thought that a man may be the enemy of other men, the enemy of other men's other moments, yet not be the enemy of a country – of fireflies, words, gardens, watercourses, zephyrs. It was amidst such thoughts that I came to a high rusty gate. Through the iron bars I made out a drive lined with poplars, and a gazebo of some kind. Suddenly, I realized two things – the first trivial, the second almost incredible: the music I had heard was coming from that gazebo, or pavillion, and the music was Chinese. That was why unconsciously I had fully given myself over to it. I do not recall whether there was a bell or whether I had to clap my hands to make my arrival known.

The sputtering of the music continued, but from the rear of the intimate house, a lantern was making its way toward me – a lantern cross-hatched and sometimes blotted out altogether by the trees, a paper lantern the shape of a drum and the colour of the moon. It was carried by a tall man. I could not see his face because the light blinded me. He opened the gate and slowly spoke to me in my own language.

'I see that the compassionate Hsi P'eng has undertaken to remedy my solitude. You will no doubt wish to see the garden?'

I recognized the name of one of our consuls, but I could only disconcertedly repeat, 'The garden?'

'The garden of forking paths.'

Something stirred in my memory, and I spoke with incomprehensible assurance.

'The garden of my ancestor Ts'ui Pen.'

'Your ancestor? Your illustrious ancestor? Please – come in.'

The dew-drenched path meandered like the paths of my childhood. We came to a library of Western and Oriental books. I recognized, bound in yellow silk, several handwritten volumes of the Lost Encyclopedia compiled by the third emperor of the Luminous Dynasty but never printed. The disk on the gramophone revolved near a bronze phoenix. I also recall a vase of *famille rose* and another, earlier by several hundred years, of that blue colour our artificers copied from the potters of ancient Persia . . .

Stephen Albert, with a smile, regarded me. He was, as I have said, quite tall, with sharp features, grey eyes, and a grey beard. There was something priestlike about him, somehow, but something sailor-like as well; later he told me he had been a missionary in Tientsin 'before aspiring to be a Sinologist.'

We sat down, I on a long low divan, he with his back to the window and a tall circular clock. I figured that my pursuer, Richard Madden, could not possibly arrive for at least an hour. My irrevocable decision could wait.

'An amazing life, Ts'ui Pen's,' Stephen Albert said. 'Governor of the province in which he had been born, a man learned in astronomy, astrology, and the unwearying interpretation of canonical books, a chess player, a renowned poet and calligrapher – he abandoned it all in order to compose a book and a labyrinth. He renounced the pleasures of oppression, justice, the populous marriage bed, banquets, and even erudition in order to sequester himself for thirteen years in the Pavillion of Limpid Solitude. Upon his death, his heirs found nothing but chaotic manuscripts. The family, as you perhaps are aware, were about to deliver them to the fire, but his counsellor – a Taoist or Buddhist monk – insisted upon publishing them.'

'To this day,' I replied, 'we who are descended from Ts'ui Pen execrate that monk. It was senseless to publish those manuscripts. The book is a contradictory jumble of irresolute drafts. I once examined it myself; in the third chapter the hero dies, yet in the fourth he is alive again. As for Ts'ui Pen's other labor, his Labyrinth . . .'

'Here is the Labyrinth,' Albert said, gesturing towards a tall lacquered writing cabinet.

'An ivory labyrinth!' I exclaimed. 'A very small sort of labyrinth . . .'

'A labyrinth of symbols,' he corrected me. 'An invisible labyrinth of time. I, an English barbarian, have somehow been chosen to unveil the diaphanous mystery. Now, more than a hundred years after the fact, the precise details are irrecoverable, but it is not difficult to surmise what happened. Ts'ui Pen must at one point have remarked, "I shall retire to write a book," and at another point, "I shall retire to construct a labyrinth." Everyone pictured two projects; it occurred to no one that book and labyrinth were one and the same. The Pavillion of Limpid Solitude was erected in the centre of a garden that was, perhaps, most intricately laid out; that fact might well have suggested a physical labyrinth. Ts'ui Pen died; no one in all the wide lands that had been his could find the labyrinth. The novel's confusion – confusedness, I mean, of course – suggested to me that it was that labyrinth. Two circumstances lent me the final solution of the problem – one, the curious legend that Ts'ui Pen had intended to construct a labyrinth which was truly infinite, and two, a fragment of a letter I discovered.'

Albert stood. His back was turned to me for several moments; he opened a drawer in the black-and-gold writing cabinet. He turned back with a paper that had once been crimson but was now pink and delicate and rectangular. It was written in Ts'ui Pen's renowned calligraphy. Eagerly yet uncomprehendingly I read the words that a man of my own lineage had written with painstaking brushstrokes: *I leave to several futures (not to all) my garden of forking paths.* I wordlessly handed the paper back to Albert. He continued:

'Before unearthing this letter, I had wondered how a book could be infinite. The only way I could surmise was that it be a cyclical, or circular, volume, a volume whose last page would be identical to the first, so that one might go on indefinitely. I also recalled that night at the centre of the *1001 Nights,* when the queen Scheherazade (through some magical distractedness on the part of the copyist) begins to retell, verbatim, the story of the 1001 Nights, with the risk of returning once again to the night on which she is telling it – and so on, *ad infinitum.* I also pictured to myself a platonic, hereditary sort of work, passed down from father to son, in which each new individual would add a chapter or with reverent care correct his elders' pages. These imaginings amused and distracted me, but none of them seemed to correspond even remotely to Ts'ui Pen's contradictory chapters. As I was floundering about in the mire of these perplexities, I was sent from Oxford the document you have just examined. I paused, as you may well imagine, at the sentence "I leave to several futures (not to all) my garden of forking paths." Almost instantly, I saw it – the garden of forking paths was the chaotic novel; the phrase "several futures (not all)" suggested to me the image of a forking in *time,* rather than in space. A full rereading of the book confirmed my theory. In all fictions, each time a man meets diverse alternatives, he chooses one and eliminates the others; in the work of the virtually impossible-to-disentangle Ts'ui Pen, the character chooses – simultaneously – all of them. *He creates,* thereby, "several futures," several *times,* which themselves proliferate and fork. That is the explanation for the novel's contradictions. Fang, let us say, has a secret; a stranger knocks at his door; Fang decides to kill him. Naturally, there are various possible outcomes – Fang can kill the intruder, the intruder can kill Fang, they can both live, they can both be killed, and so on. In Ts'ui Pen's novel, *all* the outcomes in fact occur; each is the starting point for further bifurcations. Once in a while, the paths of that labyrinth converge: for example, you come to this house, but in one of the possible pasts you are my enemy, in another my friend. If you can bear my incorrigible pronunciation, we shall read a few pages.'

His face, in the vivid circle of the lamp, was undoubtedly that of an old man, though with something indomitable and even immortal about it. He read with slow precision two versions of a single epic chapter. In the first, an army marches off to battle through a mountain wilderness; the horror of the rocks and darkness inspires in them a disdain for life, and they go on to an easy victory. In the second, the same army passes through a palace in which a ball is being held; the brilliant battle seems to them a continuation of the *fête,* and they win it easily.

I listened with honourable veneration to those ancient fictions, which were themselves perhaps not as remarkable as the fact that a man of my blood had invented them and a man of a distant empire was restoring them to me on an island in the West in the course of a desperate mission. I recall the final words, repeated in each version like some secret commandment: 'Thus the heroes fought, their admirable hearts calm, their swords violent, they themselves resigned to killing and to dying.'

From that moment on, I felt all about me and within my obscure body an invisible, intangible pullulation – not that of the divergent, parallel, and finally coalescing armies, but an agitation more inaccessible, more inward than that, yet one those armies somehow prefigured. Albert went on:

'I do not believe that your venerable ancestor played at idle variations. I cannot think it probable that he would sacrifice thirteen years to the infinite performance of a rhetorical exercise. In your country, the novel is a subordinate genre; at that time it was a genre beneath contempt. Ts'ui Pen was a novelist of genius, but he was also a man of letters, and surely would not have considered himself a mere novelist. The testimony of his contemporaries proclaims his metaphysical, mystical leanings – and his life is their fullest confirmation. Philosophical debate consumes a good part of his novel. I know that of all problems, none disturbed him, none gnawed at him like the unfathomable problem of time. How strange, then, that that problem should be the *only* one that does not figure in the pages of his *Garden*. He never even uses the word. How do you explain that wilful omission?'

I proposed several solutions – all unsatisfactory. We discussed them; finally, Stephen Albert said:

'In a riddle whose answer is chess, what is the only word that must not be used?'

I thought for a moment.

'The word "chess,"' I replied.

'Exactly,' Albert said. '*The Garden of Forking Paths* is a huge riddle, or parable, whose subject is time; that secret purpose forbids Ts'ui Pen the merest mention of its name. To *always* omit one word, to employ awkward metaphors and obvious circumlocutions, is perhaps the most emphatic way of calling attention to that word. It is, at any rate, the tortuous path chosen by the devious Ts'ui Pen at each and every one of the turnings of his inexhaustible novel. I have compared hundreds of manuscripts, I have corrected the errors introduced through the negligence of copyists, I have reached a hypothesis for the plan of that chaos, I have reestablished, or believe I've reestablished, its fundamental order – I have translated the entire work; and I know that not once does the word "time" appear. The explanation is obvious: *The Garden of Forking Paths* is an incomplete, but not false, image of the universe as conceived by Ts'ui Pen. Unlike Newton and Schopenhauer, your ancestor did not believe in a uniform and absolute time; he believed in an infinite series of times, a growing, dizzying web of divergent, convergent, and parallel times. That fabric of times that approach one another, fork, are snipped off, or are simply unknown for centuries, contains *all* possibilities. In most of those times, we do not exist; in some, you exist but I do not; in others, I do and you do not; in others still, we both do. In this one, which the favouring hand of chance has dealt me, you have come to my home; in another, when you come through my garden you find me dead; in another, I say these same words, but I am an error, a ghost.'

'In all,' I said, not without a tremble, 'I am grateful for, and I venerate, your re-creation of the garden of Ts'ui Pen.'

'Not in all,' he whispered with a smile. 'Time forks, perpetually, into countless futures. In one of them, I am your enemy.'

I felt again that pullulation I have mentioned. I sensed that the dew-drenched garden that surrounded the house was saturated, infinitely, with invisible persons. Those persons were Albert and myself – secret, busily at work, multiform – in other dimensions of time. I raised my eyes and the gossamer nightmare faded. In the yellow-and-black garden there was but a single man – but that man was as mighty as a statue, and that man was coming down the path, and he was Capt. Richard Madden.

'The future is with us,' I replied, 'but I am your friend. May I look at the letter again?'

Albert rose once again. He stood tall as he opened the drawer of the tall writing cabinet; he turned his back to me for a moment. I had cocked the revolver. With utmost care, I fired. Albert fell without a groan, without a sound, on the instant. I swear that he died instantly – one clap of thunder.

The rest is unreal, insignificant. Madden burst into the room and arrested me. I have been sentenced to hang. I have most abhorrently triumphed: I have communicated to Berlin the secret name of the city to be attacked. Yesterday it was bombed – I read about it in the same newspapers that posed to all of

England the enigma of the murder of the eminent Sinologist Stephen Albert by a stranger, Yu Tsun. The Leader solved the riddle. He knew that my problem was how to report (over the deafening noise of the war) the name of the city named Albert, and that the only way I could find was murdering a person of that name. He does not know (no one can know) my endless contrition, and my weariness.

Funes, His Memory

I recall him (though I have no right to speak that
sacred verb – only one man on earth did, and that
man is dead) holding a dark passionflower in his
hand, seeing it as it had never been seen, even had it
been stared at from the first light of dawn till the last
light of evening for an entire lifetime. I recall him – his
taciturn face, its Indian features, its extraordinary
remoteness – behind the cigarette. I recall (I think) the
slender, leather-braider's fingers. I recall near those
hands a *mate* cup, with the coat of arms of the Banda
Oriental. I recall, in the window of his house, a yellow
straw blind with some vague painted lake scene. I
clearly recall his voice – the slow, resentful, nasal voice
of the toughs of those days, without the Italian sibi-
lants one hears today. I saw him no more than three
times, the last time in 1887 . . . I applaud the idea that
all of us who had dealings with the man should write

something about him; my testimony will perhaps be the briefest (and certainly the slightest) account in the volume that you are to publish, but it can hardly be the least impartial. Unfortunately I am Argentine, and so congenitally unable to produce the dithyramb that is the obligatory genre in Uruguay, especially when the subject is an Uruguayan. *Highbrow, dandy, city slicker* – Funes did not utter those insulting words, but I know with reasonable certainty that to him I represented those misfortunes. Pedro Leandro Ipuche has written that Funes was a precursor of the race of supermen – 'a maverick and vernacular Zarathustra' – and I will not argue the point, but one must not forget that he was also a street tough from Fray Bentos, with certain incorrigible limitations.

My first recollection of Funes is quite clear. I see him one afternoon in March or February of '84. That year, my father had taken me to spend the summer in Fray Bentos. I was coming back from the ranch in San Francisco with my cousin Bernardo Haedo. We were riding along on our horses, singing merrily – and being on horseback was not the only reason for my cheerfulness. After a sultry day, a huge slate-colored storm, fanned by the south wind, had curtained the sky. The wind flailed the trees wildly, and I was filled with the fear (the hope) that we would be surprised in the open countryside by the elemental water. We ran a kind of race against the storm. We turned into the deep bed of a narrow street that ran between two brick sidewalks built high up off the ground. It had suddenly got dark; I heard quick, almost secret footsteps above me – I raised my eyes and saw a boy running along the narrow, broken sidewalk high above, as though running along the top of a narrow, broken wall. I recall the short, baggy trousers – like a gaucho's – that he wore, the straw-soled cotton slippers, the cigarette in the hard visage, all stark against the now limitless storm cloud. Unexpectedly, Bernardo shouted out to him – *What's the time, Ireneo?* Without consulting the sky, without a second's pause, the boy replied, *Four minutes till eight, young Bernardo Juan Francisco.* The voice was shrill and mocking.

I am so absentminded that I would never have given a second thought to the exchange I've just reported had my attention not been called to it by my cousin, who was prompted by a certain local pride and the desire to seem unfazed by the other boy's trinomial response.

He told me that the boy in the narrow street was one Ireneo Funes, and that he was known for certain eccentricities, among them shying away from people and always knowing what time it was, like a clock. He added that Ireneo was the son of a village ironing woman, María Clementina Funes, and that while some people said his father was a doctor in the salting house (an Englishman named O'Connor), others said he broke horses or drove oxcarts for a living over in the department of Salto. The boy lived with his mother, my cousin told me, around the corner from Villa Los Laureles.

In '85 and '86, we spent the summer in Montevideo; it was not until '87 that I returned to Fray Bentos. Naturally, I asked about everybody I knew, and finally about 'chronometric Funes.' I was told he'd been bucked off a half-broken horse on the ranch in San Francisco and had been left hopelessly crippled. I recall the sensation of unsettling magic that this news gave me: The only time I'd seen him, we'd been coming home on horseback from the ranch in San Francisco, and he had been walking along a high place. This new event, told by my cousin Bernardo, struck me as very much like a dream confected out of elements of the past. I was told that Funes never stirred from his cot, his eyes fixed on the fig tree behind the house or on a spiderweb. At dusk, he would let himself be carried to the window. He was such a proud young man that he pretended that his disastrous fall had actually been fortunate . . . Twice I saw him, on his cot behind the iron-barred window that crudely underscored his prisonerlike state – once lying motionless, with his eyes closed; the second time motionless as well, absorbed in the contemplation of a fragrant switch of artemisia.

It was not without some self-importance that about that same time I had embarked upon a systematic study of Latin. In my suitcase I had brought with me Lhomond's *De viris illustribus,* Quicherat's *Thesaurus,* Julius Caesar's commentaries, and an odd-numbered volume of Pliny's *Naturalis historia* – a work which exceeded (and still exceeds) my modest abilities as a Latinist. There are no secrets in a small town; Ireneo, in his house on the outskirts of the town, soon learned of the arrival of those outlandish books. He sent me a flowery, sententious letter, reminding me of our 'lamentably ephemeral' meeting 'on the seventh of February, 1884' He dwelt briefly, elegiacally, on the 'glorious services' that my uncle, Gregorio Haedo, who had died that same year, 'had rendered to his two motherlands in the valiant Battle of Ituzaingó,' and then he begged that I lend him one of the books I had brought, along with a dictionary 'for a full understanding of the text, since I must plead ignorance of Latin.' He promised to return the books to me in good condition, and 'straightway.' The penmanship was perfect, the letters exceptionally well formed; the spelling was that recommended by Andrés Bello: *i* for *y*, *j* for *g*. At first, of course, I thought it was some sort of joke. My cousins assured me it was not, that this 'was just ... just Ireneo.' I didn't know whether to attribute to brazen conceit, ignorance, or stupidity the idea that hard-won Latin needed no more teaching than a dictionary could give; in order to fully disabuse Funes, I sent him Quicherat's *Gradus ad Parnassum* and the Pliny.

On February 14, I received a telegram from Buenos Aires urging me to return home immediately; my father was 'not at all well.' God forgive me, but the prestige of being the recipient of an urgent telegram, the desire to communicate to all of Fray Bentos the contradiction between the negative form of the news and the absoluteness of the adverbial phrase, the temptation to dramatize my grief by feigning a virile stoicism – all this perhaps distracted me from any possibility of real pain. As I packed my bag, I realized that I didn't have the *Gradus ad Parnassum* and the first volume of Pliny. The *Saturn* was to sail the next morning; that evening, after dinner, I walked over to Funes' house. I was amazed that the evening was no less oppressive than the day had been.

At the honest little house, Funes' mother opened the door.

She told me that Ireneo was in the back room. I shouldn't be surprised if I found the room dark, she told me, since Ireneo often spent his off hours without lighting the candle. I walked across the tiled patio and down the little hallway farther on, and came to the second patio. There was a grapevine; the darkness seemed to me virtually total. Then suddenly I heard Ireneo's high, mocking voice. The voice was speaking Latin; with morbid pleasure, the voice emerging from the shadows was reciting a speech or a prayer or an incantation. The Roman syllables echoed in the patio of hard-packed earth; my trepidation made me think them incomprehensible, and endless; later, during the enormous conversation of that night, I learned they were the first paragraph of the twenty-fourth chapter of the seventh book of Pliny's *Naturalis historia*. The subject of that chapter is memory; the last words were *ut nihil non iisdem verbis redderetur auditum*.

Without the slightest change of voice, Ireneo told me to come in. He was lying on his cot, smoking. I don't think I saw his face until the sun came up the next morning; when I look back, I believe I recall the momentary glow of his cigarette. His room smelled vaguely musty. I sat down; I told him about my telegram and my father's illness.

I come now to the most difficult point in my story, a story whose only *raison d'être* (as my readers should be told from the outset) is that dialogue half a century ago. I will not attempt to reproduce the words of it, which are now forever irrecoverable. Instead, I will summarize, faithfully, the many things Ireneo told me. Indirect discourse is distant and weak; I know that I am sacrificing the effectiveness of my tale. I only ask that my readers try to hear in their imagination the broken and staccato periods that astounded me that night.

Ireneo began by enumerating, in both Latin and

Spanish, the cases of prodigious memory cataloged in the *Naturalis historia:* Cyrus, the king of Persia, who could call all the soldiers in his armies by name; Mithridates Eupator, who meted out justice in the twenty-two languages of the kingdom over which he ruled; Simonides, the inventor of the art of memory; Metrodorus, who was able faithfully to repeat what he had heard, though it be but once. With obvious sincerity, Ireneo said he was amazed that such cases were thought to be amazing. He told me that before that rainy afternoon when the blue roan had bucked him off, he had been what every man was – blind, deaf, befuddled, and virtually devoid of memory. (I tried to remind him how precise his perception of time, his memory for proper names had been – he ignored me.) He had lived, he said, for nineteen years as though in a dream: he looked without seeing, heard without listening, forgot everything, or virtually everything. When he fell, he'd been knocked unconscious; when he came to again, the present was so rich, so clear, that it was almost unbearable, as were his oldest and even his most trivial memories. It was shortly afterward that he learned he was crippled; of that fact he hardly took notice. He reasoned (or felt) that immobility was a small price to pay. Now his perception and his memory were perfect.

With one quick look, you and I perceive three wineglasses on a table; Funes perceived every grape that had been pressed into the wine and all the stalks and tendrils of its vineyard. He knew the forms of the clouds in the southern sky on the morning of April 30, 1882, and he could compare them in his memory with the veins in the marbled binding of a book he had seen only once, or with the feathers of spray lifted by an oar on the Río Negro on the eve of the Battle of Quebracho. Nor were those memories simple – every visual image was linked to muscular sensations, thermal sensations, and so on. He was able to reconstruct every dream, every daydream he had ever had. Two or three times he had reconstructed an entire day; he had never once erred or faltered, but each reconstruction had itself taken an entire day. *'I, myself, alone, have more memories than all mankind since the world began,'* he said to me. And also: *'My dreams are like other people's waking hours.'* And again, toward dawn: *'My memory, sir, is like a garbage heap.'* A circle drawn on a blackboard, a right triangle, a rhombus – all these are forms we can fully intuit;

Ireneo could do the same with the stormy mane of a young colt, a small herd of cattle on a mountainside, a flickering fire and its uncountable ashes, and the many faces of a dead man at a wake. I have no idea how many stars he saw in the sky.

Those are the things he told me; neither then nor later have I ever doubted them. At that time there were no cinematographers, no phonographs; it nevertheless strikes me as implausible, even incredible, that no one ever performed an experiment with Funes. But then, all our lives we postpone everything that can be postponed; perhaps we all have the certainty, deep inside, that we are immortal and that sooner or later every man will do everything, know all there is to know.

The voice of Funes, from the darkness, went on talking.

He told me that in 1886 he had invented a numbering system original with himself, and that within a very few days he had passed the twenty-four thousand mark. He had not written it down, since anything he thought, even once, remained ineradicably with him. His original motivation, I think, was his irritation that the thirty-three Uruguayan patriots should

equire two figures and three words rather than a
single figure, a single word. He then applied this mad
principle to the other numbers. Instead of seven thou-
and thirteen (7013), he would say, for instance,
Máximo Pérez'; instead of seven thousand fourteen
7014), 'the railroad'; other numbers were 'Luis
Melián Lafinur,' 'Olimar,' 'sulfur,' 'clubs,' 'the whale,'
gas,' 'a stewpot,' 'Napoleon,' 'Agustín de Vedia.'
nstead of five hundred (500), he said 'nine.' Every
word had a particular figure attached to it, a sort of
marker; the later ones were extremely complicated . . .
tried to explain to Funes that his rhapsody of uncon-
nected words was exactly the opposite of a number
system. I told him that when one said '365' one said
three hundreds, six tens, and five ones,' a breakdown
mpossible with the 'numbers' *Nigger Timoteo* or *a
ponchoful of meat*. Funes either could not or would
not understand me.

In the seventeenth century, Locke postulated (and
condemned) an impossible language in which each
ndividual thing – every stone, every bird, every
branch – would have its own name; Funes once contemplated a similar language, but discarded the idea
is too general, too ambiguous. The truth was, Funes

remembered not only every leaf of every tree in every patch of forest, but every time he had perceived or imagined that leaf. He resolved to reduce every one of his past days to some seventy thousand recollections, which he would then define by numbers. Two considerations dissuaded him: the realization that the task was interminable, and the realization that it was pointless. He saw that by the time he died he would still not have finished classifying all the memories of his childhood.

The two projects I have mentioned (an infinite vocabulary for the natural series of numbers, and a pointless mental catalog of all the images of his memory) are foolish, even preposterous, but they reveal a certain halting grandeur. They allow us to glimpse, or to infer, the dizzying world that Funes lived in. Funes, we must not forget, was virtually incapable of general, platonic ideas. Not only was it difficult for him to see that the generic symbol 'dog' took in all the dissimilar individuals of all shapes and sizes, it irritated him that the 'dog' of three-fourteen in the afternoon, seen in profile, should be indicated by the same noun as the dog of three-fifteen, seen frontally. His own face in the mirror, his own hands, surprised him every time he saw them. Swift wrote that the emperor of Lilliput could perceive the movement of the minute hand of a clock; Funes could continually perceive the quiet advances of corruption, of tooth decay, of weariness. He saw – he *noticed* – the progress of death, of humidity. He was the solitary, lucid spectator of a multiform, momentaneous, and almost unbearably precise world. Babylon, London, and New York dazzle mankind's imagination with their fierce splendor; no one in the populous towers or urgent avenues of those cities has ever felt the heat and pressure of a reality as inexhaustible as that which battered Ireneo, day and night, in his poor South American hinterland. It was hard for him to sleep. To sleep is to take one's mind from the world; Funes, lying on his back on his cot, in the dimness of his room, could picture every crack in the wall, every molding of the precise houses that surrounded him. (I repeat that the most trivial of his memories was more detailed, more vivid than our own perception of a physical pleasure or a physical torment.) Off toward the east, in an area that had not yet been cut up into city blocks, there were new houses, unfamiliar to Ireneo. He pictured them to himself as black,

35

compact, made of homogeneous shadow; he would turn his head in that direction to sleep. He would also imagine himself at the bottom of a river, rocked (and negated) by the current.

He had effortlessly learned English, French, Portuguese, Latin. I suspect, nevertheless, that he was not very good at thinking. To think is to ignore (or forget) differences, to generalize, to abstract. In the teeming world of Ireneo Funes there was nothing but particulars – and they were virtually *immediate* particulars.

The leery light of dawn entered the patio of packed earth.

It was then that I saw the face that belonged to the voice that had been talking all night long. Ireneo was nineteen, he had been born in 1868; he looked to me as monumental as bronze – older than Egypt, older than the prophecies and the pyramids. I was struck by the thought that every word I spoke, every expression of my face or motion of my hand would endure in his implacable memory; I was rendered clumsy by the fear of making pointless gestures.

Ireneo Funes died in 1889 of pulmonary congestion.

The Library of Babel

By this art you may contemplate the variation of the 23 letters . . .

Anatomy of Melancholy, *Pt. 2, Sec. II, Mem. IV*

The universe (which others call the Library) is composed of an indefinite, perhaps infinite number of hexagonal galleries. In the center of each gallery is a ventilation shaft, bounded by a low railing. From any hexagon one can see the floors above and below – one after another, endlessly. The arrangement of the galleries is always the same: Twenty bookshelves, five to each side, line four of the hexagon's six sides; the height of the bookshelves, floor to ceiling, is hardly greater than the height of a normal librarian. One of the hexagon's free sides opens onto a narrow sort of vestibule, which in turn opens onto another gallery, identical to the first – identical in fact to all. To the left and right of the vestibule are two tiny compartments. One is for sleeping, upright; the other, for satisfying one's physical necessities. Through this space, too, there passes a spiral staircase, which winds upward and downward into the remotest distance. In the vestibule there is a mirror, which faithfully duplicates appearances. Men often infer from this mirror that the Library is not infinite – if it were, what need would there be for that illusory replication? I prefer to dream that burnished surfaces are a figuration and promise of the infinite . . . Light is provided by certain spherical fruits that bear the name 'bulbs.' There are two of these bulbs in each hexagon, set crosswise. The light they give is insufficient, and unceasing.

Like all the men of the Library, in my younger days I traveled; I have journeyed in quest of a book, perhaps the catalog of catalogs. Now that my eyes can hardly make out what I myself have written, I am preparing to die, a few leagues from the hexagon where I was born. When I am dead, compassionate hands will throw me over the railing; my tomb will be the unfathomable air, my body will sink for ages, and will decay and dissolve in the wind engendered by my fall, which shall be infinite. I declare that the Library is endless. Idealists argue that the hexagonal rooms are the necessary shape of absolute space, or at least of our *perception* of space. They argue that a triangular or pentagonal chamber is inconceivable. (Mystics claim that their ecstasies reveal to them a circular chamber containing an enormous circular book with a continuous spine that goes completely around the walls. But their testimony is suspect, their words obscure. That cyclical book is God.) Let it suffice for the moment that I repeat the classic dictum: *The Library is a sphere whose exact center is any hexagon and whose circumference is unattainable.*

Each wall of each hexagon is furnished with five bookshelves; each bookshelf holds thirty-two books identical in format; each book contains four hundred ten pages; each page, forty lines; each line, approximately eighty black letters. There are also letters on the front cover of each book; those letters neither indicate nor prefigure what the pages inside will say. I am aware that that lack of correspondence once struck men as mysterious. Before summarizing the solution of the mystery (whose discovery, in spite of its tragic consequences, is perhaps the most important event in all history), I wish to recall a few axioms.

First: *The Library has existed* ab æternitate. That truth, whose immediate corollary is the future eternity of the world, no rational mind can doubt. Man, the imperfect librarian, may be the work of chance or of malevolent demiurges; the universe, with its elegant appointments – its bookshelves, its enigmatic books, its indefatigable staircases for the traveler, and its water closets for the seated librarian – can only be the handiwork of a god. In order to grasp the distance that separates the human and the divine, one has only to compare these crude trembling symbols which my fallible hand scrawls on the cover of a book with the organic letters inside – neat, delicate, deep black, and inimitably symmetrical.

Second: *There are twenty-five orthographic symbols.** That discovery enabled mankind, three hundred years ago, to formulate a general theory of the Library and

---

* The original manuscript has neither numbers nor capital letters; punctuation is limited to the comma and the period. Those two marks, the space, and the twenty-two letters of the alphabet are the twenty-five sufficient symbols that our unknown author is referring to. [Ed. note.]

thereby satisfactorily solve the riddle that no conjecture had been able to divine – the formless and chaotic nature of virtually all books. One book, which my father once saw in a hexagon in circuit 15–94, consisted of the letters M C V perversely repeated from the first line to the last. Another (much consulted in this zone) is a mere labyrinth of letters whose penultimate page contains the phrase *O Time thy pyramids*. This much is known: For every rational line or forthright statement there are leagues of senseless cacophony, verbal nonsense, and incoherency. (I know of one semibarbarous zone whose librarians repudiate the 'vain and superstitious habit' of trying to find sense in books, equating such a quest with attempting to find meaning in dreams or in the chaotic lines of the palm of one's hand ... They will acknowledge that the inventors of writing imitated the twenty-five natural symbols, but contend that that adoption was fortuitous, coincidental, and that books in themselves have no meaning. That argument, as we shall see, is not entirely fallacious.)

For many years it was believed that those impenetrable books were in ancient or far-distant languages. It is true that the most ancient peoples, the first librarians, employed a language quite different from the one we speak today; it is true that a few miles to the right, our language devolves into dialect and that ninety floors above, it becomes incomprehensible. All of that, I repeat, is true – but four hundred ten pages of unvarying M C V's cannot belong to any language, however dialectal or primitive it may be. Some have suggested that each letter influences the next, and that the value of M C V on page 71, line 3, is not the value of the same series on another line of another page, but that vague thesis has not met with any great acceptance. Others have mentioned the possibility of codes; that conjecture has been universally accepted, though not in the sense in which its originators formulated it.

Some five hundred years ago, the chief of one of the upper hexagons* came across a book as jumbled as all the others, but containing almost two pages of homogeneous lines. He showed his find to a traveling

---

* In earlier times, there was one man for every three hexagons. Suicide and diseases of the lung have played havoc with that proportion. An unspeakably melancholy memory: I have sometimes traveled for nights on end, down corridors and polished staircases, without coming across a single librarian.

decipherer, who told him that the lines were written in Portuguese; others said it was Yiddish. Within the century experts had determined what the language actually was: a Samoyed-Lithuanian dialect of Guaraní, with inflections from classical Arabic. The content was also determined: the rudiments of combinatory analysis, illustrated with examples of endlessly repeating variations. Those examples allowed a librarian of genius to discover the fundamental law of the Library. This philosopher observed that all books, however different from one another they might be, consist of identical elements: the space, the period, the comma, and the twenty-two letters of the alphabet. He also posited a fact which all travelers have since confirmed: *In all the Library, there are no two identical books.* From those incontrovertible premises, the librarian deduced that the Library is 'total' – perfect, complete, and whole – and that its bookshelves contain all possible combinations of the twenty-two orthographic symbols (a number which, though unimaginably vast, is not infinite) – that is, all that is able to be expressed, in every language. *All* – the detailed history of the future, the autobiographies of the archangels, the faithful catalog of the Library, thousands and thousands of false catalogs, the proof of the falsity of those false catalogs, a proof of the falsity of the *true* catalog, the gnostic gospel of Basilides, the commentary upon that gospel, the commentary on the commentary on that gospel, the true story of your death, the translation of every book into every language, the interpolations of every book into all books, the treatise Bede could have written (but did not) on the mythology of the Saxon people, the lost books of Tacitus.

When it was announced that the Library contained all books, the first reaction was unbounded joy. All men felt themselves the possessors of an intact and secret treasure. There was no personal problem, no world problem, whose eloquent solution did not exist – somewhere in some hexagon. The universe was justified; the universe suddenly became congruent with the unlimited width and breadth of humankind's hope. At that period there was much talk of The Vindications – books of *apologiæ* and prophecies that would vindicate for all time the actions of every person in the universe and that held wondrous arcana for men's futures. Thousands of greedy individuals abandoned their sweet native hexagons and rushed downstairs, upstairs, spurred by the vain desire to find their Vindication. These pilgrims squabbled in the narrow corridors, muttered dark imprecations, strangled one another on the divine staircases, threw deceiving volumes down ventilation shafts, were themselves hurled to their deaths by men of distant regions. Others went insane . . . The Vindications do exist (I have seen two of them, which refer to persons in the future, persons perhaps not imaginary), but those who went in quest of them failed to recall that the chance of a man's finding his own Vindication, or some perfidious version of his own, can be calculated to be zero.

At that same period there was also hope that the fundamental mysteries of mankind – the origin of the Library and of time – might be revealed. In all likelihood those profound mysteries can indeed be explained in words; if the language of the philosophers is not sufficient, then the multiform Library must surely have produced the extraordinary language that is required, together with the words and grammar of that language. For four centuries, men have been scouring the hexagons . . . There are official searchers, the 'inquisitors.' I have seen them about their tasks: they arrive exhausted at some hexagon, they talk about a staircase that nearly killed them – some steps were missing – they speak with the librarian about galleries and staircases, and, once in a while, they take up the nearest book and leaf through it, searching for disgraceful or dishonorable words. Clearly, no one expects to discover anything.

That unbridled hopefulness was succeeded, naturally enough, by a similarly disproportionate depression. The certainty that some bookshelf in some hexagon contained precious books, yet that those precious books were forever out of reach, was almost unbearable. One blasphemous sect proposed that the searches be discontinued and that all men shuffle letters and symbols until those canonical books, through some improbable stroke of chance, had been constructed. The authorities were forced to issue strict orders. The sect disappeared, but in my childhood I have seen old men who for long periods would hide in the latrines with metal disks and a forbidden dice cup, feebly mimicking the divine disorder.

Others, going about it in the opposite way, thought the first thing to do was eliminate all worthless books.

They would invade the hexagons, show credentials that were not always false, leaf disgustedly through a volume, and condemn entire walls of books. It is to their hygienic, ascetic rage that we lay the senseless loss of millions of volumes. Their name is execrated today, but those who grieve over the 'treasures' destroyed in that frenzy overlook two widely acknowledged facts: One, that the Library is so huge that any reduction by human hands must be infinitesimal. And two, that each book is unique and irreplaceable, but (since the Library is total) there are always several hundred thousand imperfect facsimiles – books that differ by no more than a single letter, or a comma. Despite general opinion, I daresay that the consequences of the depredations committed by the Purifiers have been exaggerated by the horror those same fanatics inspired. They were spurred on by the holy zeal to reach – someday, through unrelenting effort – the books of the Crimson Hexagon – books smaller than natural books, books omnipotent, illustrated, and magical.

We also have knowledge of another superstition from that period: belief in what was termed the Book-Man. On some shelf in some hexagon, it was argued, there must exist a book that is the cipher and perfect compendium *of all other books,* and some librarian must have examined that book; this librarian is analogous to a god. In the language of this zone there are still vestiges of the sect that worshiped that distant librarian. Many have gone in search of Him. For a hundred years, men beat every possible path – and every path in vain. How was one to locate the idolized secret hexagon that sheltered Him? Someone proposed searching by regression: To locate book A, first consult book B, which tells where book A can be found; to locate book B, first consult book C, and so on, to infinity . . . It is in ventures such as these that I have squandered and spent my years. I cannot think it unlikely that there is such a total book* on some shelf in the universe. I pray to the unknown gods that some man – even a single man, tens of centuries ago – has perused and read that book. If the honor and wisdom and joy of such a reading are not to be

---

* I repeat: In order for a book to exist, it is sufficient that it be *possible.* Only the impossible is excluded. For example, no book is also a staircase, though there are no doubt books that discuss and deny and prove that possibility, and others whose structure corresponds to that of a staircase.

my own, then let them be for others. Let heaven exist, though my own place be in hell. Let me be tortured and battered and annihilated, but let there be one instant, one creature, wherein thy enormous Library may find its justification.

Infidels claim that the rule in the Library is not 'sense,' but 'non-sense,' and that 'rationality' (even humble, pure coherence) is an almost miraculous exception. They speak, I know, of 'the feverish Library, whose random volumes constantly threaten to transmogrify into others, so that they affirm all things, deny all things, and confound and confuse all things, like some mad and hallucinating deity.' Those words, which not only proclaim disorder but exemplify it as well, prove, as all can see, the infidels' deplorable taste and desperate ignorance. For while the Library contains all verbal structures, all the variations allowed by the twenty-five orthographic symbols, it includes not a single absolute piece of nonsense. It would be pointless to observe that the finest volume of all the many hexagons that I myself administer is titled *Combed Thunder,* while another is titled *The Plaster Cramp,* and another, *Axaxaxas mlö.* Those phrases, at first apparently incoherent, are undoubtedly susceptible to cryptographic or allegorical 'reading'; that reading, that justification of the words' order and existence, is itself verbal and, *ex hypothesi,* already contained somewhere in the Library. There is no combination of characters one can make – *dhcmrlchtdj,* for example – that the divine Library has not foreseen and that in one or more of its secret tongues does not hide a terrible significance. There is no syllable one can speak that is not filled with tenderness and terror, that is not, in one of those languages, the mighty name of a god. To speak is to commit tautologies. This pointless, verbose epistle already exists in one of the thirty volumes of the five bookshelves in one of the countless hexagons – as does its refutation. (A number *n* of the possible languages employ the same vocabulary; in some of them, the *symbol* 'library' possesses the correct definition 'everlasting, ubiquitous system of hexagonal galleries,' while a library – the thing – is a loaf of bread or a pyramid or something else, and the six words that define it themselves have other definitions. You who read me – are you certain you understand my language?)

Methodical composition distracts me from the

present condition of humanity. The certainty that everything has already been written annuls us, or renders us phantasmal. I know districts in which the young people prostrate themselves before books and like savages kiss their pages, though they cannot read a letter. Epidemics, heretical discords, pilgrimages that inevitably degenerate into brigandage have decimated the population. I believe I mentioned the suicides, which are more and more frequent every year. I am perhaps misled by old age and fear, but I suspect that the human species – the *only* species – teeters at the verge of extinction, yet that the Library – enlightened, solitary, infinite, perfectly unmoving, armed with precious volumes, pointless, incorruptible, and secret – will endure.

I have just written the word 'infinite.' I have not included that adjective out of mere rhetorical habit; I hereby state that it is not illogical to think that the world is infinite. Those who believe it to have limits hypothesize that in some remote place or places the corridors and staircases and hexagons may, inconceivably, end – which is absurd. And yet those who picture the world as unlimited forget that the number of possible books is *not*. I will be bold enough to suggest this solution to the ancient problem: *The Library is unlimited but periodic.* If an eternal traveler should journey in any direction, he would find after untold centuries that the same volumes are repeated in the same disorder – which, repeated, becomes order: the Order. My solitude is cheered by that elegant hope.*

Mar del Plata, 1941

* Letizia Alvarez de Toledo has observed that the vast Library is pointless; strictly speaking, all that is required is a *single volume,* of the common size, printed in nine- or ten-point type, that would consist of an infinite number of infinitely thin pages. (In the early seventeenth century, Cavalieri stated that every solid body is the superposition of an infinite number of planes.) Using that silken *vademecum* would not be easy: each apparent page would open into other similar pages; the inconceivable middle page would have no 'back.'

Death and the Compass

For Mandie Molina Vedia

Of the many problems on which Lönnrot's reckless perspicacity was exercised, none was so strange – so *rigorously* strange, one might say – as the periodic series of bloody deeds that culminated at the Villa Triste-le-Roy, amid the perpetual fragrance of the eucalyptus. It is true that Erik Lönnrot did not succeed in preventing the last crime, but he did, indisputably, foresee it. Nor did he divine the identity of Yarmolinsky's unlucky murderer, but he did perceive the evil series' secret shape and the part played in it by Red Scharlach, whose second sobriquet is Scharlach the Dandy. That criminal (like so many others) had sworn upon his honor to kill Lönnrot, but Lönnrot never allowed himself to be intimidated. He thought of himself as a reasoning machine, an

Auguste Dupin, but there was something of the adventurer in him, even something of the gambler.

The first crime occurred in the Hôtel du Nord, that tall prism sitting high above the estuary whose waters are the color of the desert. To that tower (which is notorious for uniting in itself the abhorrent whiteness of a sanatorium, the numbered divisibility of a prison, and the general appearance of a house of ill repute) there came, on December 3, the delegate from Podolsk to the Third Talmudic Congress – Dr Marcelo Yarmolinsky, a man of gray beard and gray eyes. We will never know whether he found the Hôtel du Nord to his liking; he accepted it with the ancient resignation that had allowed him to bear three years of war in the Carpathians and three thousand years of pogroms and oppression. He was given a room on R Floor, across the hall from the suite occupied – not without some splendor – by the Tetrarch of Galilee. Yarmolinsky had dinner, put off till the next day his examination of the unfamiliar city, set out his many books and very few articles of jewelry on a bureau, and, before midnight, turned off the light. (Thus testified the tetrarch's driver, who was sleeping in the adjoining room.) On the fourth, at 11:30 AM, a writer for the *Yiddische Zeitung* telephoned Yarmolinsky, but Dr Yarmolinsky did not answer. He was found lying on the floor of his room, his face by now slightly discolored, his body almost naked beneath an anachronistic cape. He was lying not far from the door to the hallway; a deep knife wound had rent his chest. A couple of hours later, in the same room, standing amid journalists, photographers, and gendarmes, police commissioner Treviranus and Lönnrot serenely discussed the problem.

'No need to go off on wild-goose chases here,' Treviranus was saying, as he brandished an imperious cigar. 'We all know that the Tetrarch of Galilee owns the finest sapphires in the world. Somebody intending to steal the sapphires broke in here by mistake. Yarmolinsky woke up, the burglar had to kill him. – What do you think?'

'Possible, but uninteresting,' Lönnrot replied. 'You will reply that reality has not the slightest obligation to be interesting. I will reply in turn that reality may get along without that obligation, but hypotheses may not. In the hypothesis that you suggest, here, on the spur of the moment, chance plays a disproportionate role. What we have here is a dead rabbi; I would prefer

55

a purely rabbinical explanation, not the imaginary bunglings of an imaginary burglar.'

Treviranus' humor darkened.

'I'm not interested in "rabbinical explanations," as you call them; what I'm interested in is catching the blackguard that stabbed this unknown man.'

'Unknown?' asked Lönnrot. 'Here are his complete works.' He gestured to the bureau with its row of tall books: *A Vindication of the Kabbalah; A Study of the Philosophy of Robert Fludd;* a literal translation of the *Sefer Yetsirah*; a *Biography of the Baal Shem; A History of the Hasidim;* a monograph in German on the Tetragrammaton; another on the divine nomenclature of the Pentateuch. The commissioner looked at them with fear, almost with revulsion. Then he laughed.

'I'm a poor Christian fellow,' he replied. 'You can take those things home with you, if you want them; I can't be wasting my time on Jewish superstitions.'

'This crime may, however, *belong* to the history of Jewish superstitions,' Lönnrot muttered.

'As Christianity does,' the writer from the *Yiddische Zeitung* added, scathingly. He was nearsighted, quite shy, and an atheist.

No one answered him. In the little typewriter, one

of the agents had found a slip of paper, with this unfinished declaration:

The first letter of the Name has been written.

Lönnrot resisted a smile. Suddenly turned bibliophile or Hebraist, he ordered one of the officers to wrap up the dead man's books, and he took them to his apartment. Then, indifferent to the police investigation, he set about studying them. One book, an octavo volume, revealed to him the teachings of Israel Baal Shem Tov, the founder of the sect of the Pious; another, the virtues and terrors of the Tetragrammaton, the ineffable name of God; yet another, the notion that God has a secret name, which (much like the crystal sphere attributed by the Persians to Alexander of Macedonia) contains His ninth attribute, the eternity – that is, immediate knowledge – of all things that shall be, are, and have been in the universe. Tradition reckons the names of God at ninety-nine; while Hebraists attribute that imperfect sum to the magical fear of even numbers, the Hasidim argue that the lacuna points toward a hundredth name – the Absolute Name.

From his erudition Lönnrot was distracted, a few

days later, by the writer from the *Yiddische Zeitung*. The young man wanted to talk about the murder; Lönnrot preferred to talk about the many names of God. The journalist filled three columns with the story that the famed detective Erik Lönnrot had taken up the study of the names of God in order to discover the name of the murderer. Lönnrot, accustomed to journalists' simplifications, did not take offense. One of those shopkeepers who have found that any given man may be persuaded to buy any given book published a popular edition of *A History of the Hasidim*.

The second crime took place on the night of January 3, in the emptiest and most godforsaken of the echoing suburbs on the western outskirts of the capital. Sometime around dawn, one of the mounted gendarmes that patrolled the solitudes of those blocks saw a man, wrapped in a poncho, lying in the doorway of an old paint factory. His hard face looked as though it were wearing a mask of blood; a deep knife wound split his chest. On the wall, across the red and yellow rhombuses, someone had chalked some words, which the gendarme spelled out to himself . . . That afternoon, Treviranus and Lönnrot made their way to the distant scene of the crime. To the left and right of their automobile, the city crumbled away; the sky expanded, and now houses held less and less importance, a brick kiln or a poplar tree more and more. They came to their miserable destination; a final alleyway lined with pink-colored walls that somehow seemed to reflect the rambunctious setting of the sun. By this time, the dead man had been identified. He was Daniel Simón Azevedo, a man of some reputation in the old slums of the Northside, where he had risen from wagon driver to election-day thug, only to degenerate thereafter into a thief and even an informer. (The singular manner of his death seemed fitting: Azevedo was the last representative of a generation of outlaws who used a knife but not a revolver.) The chalked words read as follows:

The second letter of the Name has been written.

The third crime took place on the night of February 3. A few minutes before one, the telephone rang in Commissioner Treviranus' office. Keenly secretive, the guttural voice of a man came on the line; he told the commissioner his name was Ginzberg (or Ginsburg) and said that for a reasonable fee he was willing to reveal certain details of the two sacrifices, Azevedo's and Yarmolinsky's. A cacophony of whistles and party horns drowned out the informer's voice. Then, the line went dead. Without discarding the possibility of a prank (it was carnival time, after all), Treviranus made inquiries and found that the call had come from Liverpool House, a tavern on the rue de Toulon – that brackish street shared by a popular museum of wonders and a milk store, a brothel and a company of Bible sellers. Treviranus telephoned the owner of the place – Black Finnegan, former Irish criminal now overwhelmed, almost crushed, by honesty. Finnegan told Treviranus that the last person to use the telephone in the tavern had been a tenant, one Gryphius, who'd just gone out with some friends. Treviranus drove immediately to Liverpool House. The owner had the following to say: Eight days earlier, Gryphius – a man with sharp features, a nebulous gray beard, and a nondescript black suit – had rented a room above the bar. Finnegan (who generally put the room to a use that Treviranus had no difficulty guessing) had named an exorbitant rent; Gryphius had unhesitatingly paid it. He almost never left the room; he had both lunch and dinner there and hardly ever showed his face in

the bar. That night he had come down to Finnegan's
office to make a call. A closed coupe had stopped in
front of the tavern. The driver hadn't left the driver's
seat; some of the customers recalled that he was
wearing a bear mask. Two harlequin figures got out
of the car; they were short, and no one could fail to
notice that they were drunk. They burst into Finnegan's office, party horns bleating, and threw their
arms around Gryphius, who apparently recognized
them but greeted them somewhat coldly. They
exchanged a few words in Yiddish – Gryphius in a
low, guttural voice, the harlequins in a sort of
falsetto – and then all went up to Gryphius' room.
Fifteen minutes later the three men came down again,
quite happy; Gryphius was staggering, and seemed
to be as drunk as the others. Tall and unsteady, his
head apparently spinning, he was in the middle,
between the masked harlequins. (One of the women
in the bar recalled the yellow, red, and green lozenges.) Twice he stumbled; twice the harlequins
steadied him. The three men got into the coupe and
disappeared in the direction of the nearby pier, with
its rectangular water. But just as he stepped on the
running board of the car, the last harlequin scrawled

an obscene figure and a sentence on one of the black-boards in the entryway.

Treviranus looked at the sentence, but it was almost predictable:

The last letter of the Name has been written.

Then he examined Gryphius-Ginsburg's little room. On the floor, there was a brusque star, in blood; in the corners, the remains of cigarettes, Hungarian; on a bureau, a book in Latin – Leusden's *Philologus hebræogræcus* (1739) – with several handwritten notes. Treviranus looked at it indignantly, and sent for Lönnrot. Lönnrot did not take his hat off before plunging into the book, while the commissioner interrogated the contradictory witnesses to the possible kidnapping. At four they left. Out in the twisting rue de Toulon, as they walked through the dawn's dead streamers and confetti, Treviranus said:

'What if tonight's story were a sham, a simulacrum?'

Erik Lönnrot smiled and in a grave voice read the commissioner a passage (which had been underlined) from the *Philologus'* thirty-third dissertation: *Dies Judæorum incipit a solis occasu usque ad solis occasum diei sequentis.* 'Which means,' he added, ' "The Jewish day begins at sundown and lasts until sundown of the following day." '

The other man made an attempt at irony.

'And is that the most valuable piece of information you've picked up tonight, then?'

'No. The most valuable piece of information is the word Ginsburg used.'

The afternoon papers had not overlooked these periodic deaths and disappearances. The *Cross and Sword* contrasted them with the admirable discipline and order of the last Hermetic congress; Ernst Palast of *The Martyr* denounced 'the intolerable delays of a clandestine and niggardly pogrom, which has taken three months to wipe out three Jews'; the *Yiddische Zeitung* rejected the horrifying theory of an anti-Semitic conspiracy, 'though many insightful spirits will hear of no other solution for the triple mystery'; the most famous gunman of the Southside, Dandy Red Scharlach, swore that in his territory no crime such as that had ever taken place, and he accused Police Commissioner Franz Treviranus of criminal negligence.

On March 1, this same Treviranus received an impressive-looking sealed envelope. He opened it; it contained a letter signed 'Baruch Spinoza' and a detailed map of the city, clearly torn out of a Baedeker. The letter predicted that on the third of March there would not be a fourth crime, because the paint factory in the west, the tavern on the rue de Toulon, and the Hôtel du Nord were 'the perfect points of a mystical, equilateral triangle'; red ink on the map demonstrated its regularity. Treviranus read over that argument-by-geometry resignedly and then sent both letter and map to Lönnrot's house, Lönnrot indisputably being a man who deserved this sort of claptrap.

Erik Lönnrot studied the map and letter. The three locations were indeed equidistant. Symmetry in time (December 3, January 3, February 3); symmetry in space, as well . . . Lönnrot sensed, abruptly, that he was on the brink of solving the riddle. A drawing-compass and a navigational compass completed that sudden intuition. He smiled, spoke the word Tetra-grammaton (a word he had recently acquired), and telephoned the commissioner.

'Thanks for that equilateral triangle you sent me last night. It was what I needed to solve the puzzle. Tomorrow, Friday, the perpetrators will be in prison; we can relax.'

'Then they're not planning a fourth crime?'

'It's precisely because they *are* planning a fourth crime that we can relax,' Lönnrot said as he hung up.

An hour later, he was riding on a Southern Railway train toward the abandoned Villa Triste-le-Roy. South of the city of my story flows a sluggish stream of muddy water, choked with refuse and thick with the runoff of tanneries. On the other side is a suburb filled with factories where, under the protection of a Barcelona gangster, gunmen prosper. Lönnrot smiled to think that the most famous of these criminals – Red Scharlach – would have given anything to know about his clandestine visit. Azevedo had been one of Scharlach's gang; Lönnrot considered the remote possibility that Scharlach was to be the fourth victim, but then rejected it . . . He had virtually solved the problem; the mere circumstances, the reality (names, arrests, faces, the paperwork of trial and imprisonment), held very little interest for him now. He wanted to go for a walk, he wanted a respite from the three months of sedentary investigation. He reflected that the explanation for the crimes lay in an anonymous triangle and a dusty Greek word. The mystery seemed so crystal clear to him now, he was embarrassed to have spent a hundred days on it.

The train stopped at a silent loading platform. Lönnrot got off. It was one of those deserted evenings that have the look of dawn. The air of the murky plains was wet and cold. Lönnrot began to walk cross-country. He saw dogs, he saw a van or lorry in a dead-end alleyway, he saw the horizon, he saw a silvery horse lapping at the rank water of a puddle. It was growing dark when he saw the rectangular belvedere of Villa Triste-le-Roy, which stood almost as high as the black eucalyptus trees that surrounded it. The thought occurred to him that one dawn and one sunset (an ancient glow in the east and another in the west) were all that separated him from the hour yearned for by the seekers of the Name.

A rusty fence defined the irregular perimeter of the villa's grounds. The main gate was closed. Lönnrot, with no great expectation of finding a way in, walked all the way around. Back at the impregnable gate, he stuck his hand almost mechanically between the bars and came upon the latch. The creaking of the iron startled him. With laborious passivity, the entire gate yielded.

Lönnrot made his way forward through the eucalyptus trees, treading upon confused generations of
stiff red leaves. Seen at closer quarters, the house
belonging to the Villa Triste-le-Roy abounded in
pointless symmetries and obsessive repetitions; a gla-
cial Diana in a gloomy niche was echoed by a second
Diana in a second niche; one balcony was reflected
in another; double stairways opened into a double
balustrade. A two-faced Hermes threw a monstrous
shadow. Lönnrot walked all around the outside of
the house as he had made the circuit of the villa's
grounds. He inspected everything; under the level
of the terrace, he spotted a narrow shutter.

He pushed at it; two or three marble steps
descended into a cellar. Lönnrot, who by now had a
sense of the architect's predilections, guessed that
there would be another set of steps in the opposite
wall. He found them, climbed them, raised his hands,
and opened the trapdoor out.

A glowing light led him toward a window. This he
also opened; a round yellow moon defined two leaf-
clogged fountains in the dreary garden. Lönnrot
explored the house. Through foyers that opened onto
dining rooms and on through galleries, he would

emerge into identical courtyards – often the same courtyard. He climbed dusty stairs to circular ante-chambers; he would recede infinitely in the facing mirrored walls; he wearied of opening or half opening windows that revealed to him, outside, the same desolate garden from differing heights and differing angles – inside, the furnishings in yellowing covers, chandeliers swathed in muslin. A bedchamber stopped him; there, a single flower in a porcelain vase; at the first brush of his fingertips, the ancient petals crumbled. On the second floor, on the upper-most floor, the house seemed infinite yet still growing. *The house is not so large,* he thought. *It seems larger because of its dimness, its symmetry, its mirrors, its age, my unfamiliarity with it, and this solitude.*

A stairway took him to the belvedere. The moon-light of the evening shone through the lozenges of the windows; they were yellow, red, and green. He was stopped by an astonished, dizzying recol-lection.

Two fierce, stocky men leaped upon him and dis-armed him; another, quite tall, greeted him gravely:

'You are so kind. You have saved us a night and a day.'

It was Red Scharlach. The men tied Lönnrot's hands. Lönnrot at last found his voice.

'Scharlach – *you* are looking for the secret Name?'

Scharlach stood there, impassive. He had not participated in the brief struggle, and now moved only to put out his hand for Lönnrot's revolver. But then he spoke, and Lönnrot heard in his voice a tired triumphance, a hatred as large as the universe, a sadness no smaller than that hatred.

'No,' he said. 'I am looking for something more fleeting and more perishable than that – I am looking for Erik Lönnrot. Three years ago, in a gambling den on the rue de Toulon, you arrested my brother and saw that he was sent to prison. My men rescued me from the shoot-out in a coupe, but not before I'd received a policeman's bullet in my gut. Nine days and nine nights I lay between life and death in this desolate symmetrical villa, consumed by fever, and that hateful two-faced Janus that looks toward the sunset and the dawn lent horror to my deliriums and my sleeplessness. I came to abominate my own body, I came to feel that two eyes, two hands, two lungs are as monstrous as two faces. An Irishman tried to convert me to belief in Christ; he would repeat, over and over, the goyim's saying: All roads lead to Rome. At night, my delirium would grow fat upon that metaphor: I sensed that the world was a labyrinth, impossible to escape – for all roads, even if they pretended to lead north or south, returned finally to Rome, which was also the rectangular prison where my brother lay dying, and which was also the Villa Triste-le-Roy. During those nights, I swore by the god that sees with two faces, and by all the gods of fever and of mirrors, to weave a labyrinth around the man who had imprisoned my brother. I have woven it, and it has stood firm: its materials are a dead heresiologue, a compass, an eighth-century cult, a Greek word, a dagger, the rhombuses of a paint factory . . .

'The first term of the series was given me quite by chance. With some friends of mine – among them Daniel Azevedo – I had figured out a way to steal the tetrarch's sapphires. Azevedo, however, double-crossed us; he got drunk on the money we had advanced him and pulled the job a day early. But then he got lost in that huge hotel, and sometime around two o'clock in the morning he burst into Yarmolinsky's room. Yarmolinsky, who suffered from insomnia, was sitting at his typewriter typing. As coincidence would have it, he was making some notes, or writing an article perhaps, on the Name of God; he had just typed the words *The first letter of the Name has been written.* Azevedo told him to keep quiet; Yarmolinsky put out his hand toward the bell that would wake everyone in the hotel; Azevedo stabbed him once in the chest. The movement was almost reflexive; a half century of violence had taught him that the easiest and safest way is simply to kill . . . Ten days later I learned from the *Yiddische Zeitung* that you were trying to find the key to Yarmolinsky's death among Yarmolinsky's writings. I read *A History of the Hasidim;* I learned that the reverent fear of speaking the Name of God had been the origin of the doctrine that that Name is omnipotent and occult. I learned that some Hasidim, in the quest for that secret Name, had gone so far as to commit human sacrifice . . . I realized that you would conjecture that the Hasidim had sacrificed the rabbi; I set about justifying that conjecture.

'Marcelo Yarmolinsky died on the night of December third; I chose the third of January for the second "sacrifice." Yarmolinsky died in the north; for the second "sacrifice," the death should take place in the west. Daniel Azevedo was the necessary victim. He deserved to die; he was a man that acted on impulse and he was a traitor – if he were captured, he could destroy my plan. One of my men stabbed him; in order to link his body to the first one, I wrote *The second letter of the Name has been written* across the rhombuses of the paint factory.

'The third "crime" was committed on the third of February. It was, as Treviranus guessed, a mere sham, a simulacrum. *I* am Gryphius-Ginzberg-Ginsburg; I spent one interminable week (supplemented by a tissue-thin false beard) in that perverse cubicle on the rue de Toulon, until my friends kidnapped me. Standing on the running board of the coupe, one of them scrawled on a pillar the words that you recall: *The last letter of the Name has been written.* That sentence revealed that this was a series of *three* crimes. At least that was how the man in the street interpreted it – but I had repeatedly dropped clues so that *you,* the *reasoning* Erik Lönnrot, would realize that there were actually *four.* One sign in the north, two more in the east and west, demand a fourth sign in the south – after all, the Tetragrammaton, the Name of God,

YHVH, consists of *four* letters; the harlequins and the paint manufacturer's emblem suggest *four* terms. It was I who underlined that passage in Leusden's book. The passage says that Jews compute the day from sunset to sunset; the passage therefore gives one to understand that the deaths occurred on the *fourth* of each month. It was I who sent the equilateral triangle to Treviranus. I knew you would add the missing point, the point that makes a perfect rhombus, the point that fixes the place where a precise death awaits you. I have done all this, Erik Lönnrot, planned all this, in order to draw you to the solitudes of Triste-le-Roy.'

Lönnrot avoided Scharlach's eyes. He looked at the trees and the sky subdivided into murky red, green, and yellow rhombuses. He felt a chill, and an impersonal, almost anonymous sadness. The night was dark now; from the dusty garden there rose the pointless cry of a bird. For the last time, Lönnrot considered the problem of the symmetrical, periodic murders.

'There are three lines too many in your labyrinth,' he said at last. 'I know of a Greek labyrinth that is but one straight line. So many philosophers have been lost upon that line that a mere detective might be pardoned if he became lost as well. When you hunt me down in another avatar of our lives, Scharlach, I suggest that you fake (or commit) one crime at A, a second crime at B, eight kilometers from A, then a third crime at C, four kilometers from A and B and halfway between them. Then wait for me at D, two kilometers from A and C, once again halfway between them. Kill me at D, as you are about to kill me at Triste-le-Roy.'

'The next time I kill you,' Scharlach replied, 'I promise you the labyrinth that consists of a single straight line that is invisible and endless.'

He stepped back a few steps. Then, very carefully, he fired.

1942

Tlön, Uqbar, Orbis Tertius

I owe the discovery of Uqbar to the conjunction of a mirror and an encyclopedia. The mirror troubled the far end of a hallway in a large country house on Calle Gaona, in Ramos Mejía; the encyclopedia is misleadingly titled *The Anglo-American Cyclopaedia* (New York, 1917), and is a literal (though also laggardly) reprint of the 1902 *Encyclopædia Britannica*. The event took place about five years ago.

Bioy Casares had come to dinner at my house that evening, and we had lost all track of time in a vast debate over the way one might go about composing a first-person novel whose narrator would omit or distort things and engage in all sorts of contradictions, so that a few of the book's readers – a *very* few – might divine the horrifying or banal truth. Down at that far end of the hallway, the mirror hovered, shadowing us. We discovered (very late at night such a discovery is inevitable) that there is something monstrous about mirrors. That was when Bioy remembered a saying by one of the heresiarchs of Uqbar: *Mirrors and copulation are abominable, for they multiply the number of mankind.* I asked him where he'd come across that memorable epigram, and he told me it was recorded in *The Anglo-American Cyclopaedia*, in its article on Uqbar.

The big old house (we had taken it furnished) possessed a copy of that work. On the last pages of Volume XLVI we found an article on Uppsala; on the first of Volume XLVII, 'Ural-Altaic Languages' – not a word on Uqbar. Bioy, somewhat bewildered, consulted the volumes of the Index. He tried every possible spelling: Ukbar, Ucbar, Ookbar, Oukbahr . . . all in vain. Before he left, he told me it was a region in Iraq or Asia Minor. I confess I nodded a bit uncomfortably; I surmised that that undocumented country and its anonymous heresiarch were a fiction that Bioy had invented on the spur of the moment, out of modesty, in order to justify a fine-sounding epigram. A sterile search through one of the atlases of Justus Perthes reinforced my doubt.

The next day, Bioy called me from Buenos Aires. He told me he had the article on Uqbar right in front of him – in Volume XLVI of the encyclopedia. The heresiarch's name wasn't given, but the entry did report his doctrine, formulated in words almost identical to those Bioy had quoted, though from a literary point of view perhaps inferior. Bioy had remembered its being 'copulation and mirrors are abominable,' while the text of the encyclopedia ran *For one of those gnostics, the visible universe was an illusion or, more precisely, a sophism. Mirrors and fatherhood are hateful because they multiply and proclaim it.* I told Bioy, quite truthfully, that I'd like to see that article. A few days later he brought it to me – which surprised me, because the scrupulous cartographic indices of Ritter's *Erdkunde* evinced complete and total ignorance of the existence of the name Uqbar.

The volume Bioy brought was indeed Volume XLVI of the *Anglo-American Cyclopaedia*. On both the false cover and spine, the alphabetical key to the volume's contents (Tor-Upps) was the same as ours, but instead of 917 pages, Bioy's volume had 921. Those four additional pages held the article on Uqbar – an article not contemplated (as the reader will have

noted) by the alphabetical key. We later compared
the two volumes and found that there was no further
difference between them. Both (as I believe I have
said) are reprints of the tenth edition of the *Encyclopædia Britannica*. Bioy had purchased his copy at
one of his many sales.

We read the article with some care. The passage
that Bioy had recalled was perhaps the only one that
might raise a reader's eyebrow; the rest seemed quite
plausible, very much in keeping with the general tone
of the work, even (naturally) somewhat boring.
Rereading it, however, we discovered that the rigorous writing was underlain by a basic vagueness. Of
the fourteen names that figured in the section on
geography, we recognized only three (Khorasan,
Armenia, Erzerum), all interpolated into the text
ambiguously. Of the historical names, we recognized
only one: the impostor-wizard Smerdis, and he was
invoked, really, as a metaphor. The article seemed to
define the borders of Uqbar, but its nebulous points
of reference were rivers and craters and mountain
chains of the region itself. We read, for example, that
the Axa delta and the lowlands of Tsai Khaldun mark
the southern boundary, and that wild horses breed

on the islands of the delta. That was at the top of page 918. In the section on Uqbar's history (p. 920), we learned that religious persecutions in the thirteenth century had forced the orthodox to seek refuge on those same islands, where their obelisks are still standing and their stone mirrors are occasionally unearthed. The section titled 'Language and Literature' was brief. One memorable feature: the article said that the literature of Uqbar was a literature of fantasy, and that its epics and legends never referred to reality but rather to the two imaginary realms of Mle'khnas and Tlön . . . The bibliography listed four volumes we have yet to find, though the third – Silas Haslam's *History of the Land Called Uqbar* (1874) – does figure in the catalogs published by Bernard Quaritch, Bookseller.* The first, *Lesbare und lesenswerthe Bemerkungen über das Land Ukkbar in Klein-Asien,* published in 1641, is the work of one Johannes Valentinus Andreä. That fact is significant: two or three years afterward, I came upon that name in the unexpected pages of De Quincey (*Writings,* Vol. XIII), where I learned that it belonged to a German theologian who

---

* Haslam was also the author of *A General History of Labyrinths.*

in the early seventeenth century described an imagin
ary community, the Rosy Cross – which other men
later founded, in imitation of his foredescription.

That night, Bioy and I paid a visit to the National
Library, where we pored in vain through atlases, cata
logs, the yearly indices published by geographical
societies, the memoirs of travelers and historians – no
one had ever been in Uqbar. Nor did the general
index in Bioy's copy of the encyclopedia contain that
name. The next day, Carlos Mastronardi (whom I
had told about all this) spotted the black-and-gold
spines of the *Anglo-American Cyclopaedia* in a book
shop at the corner of Corrientes and Talcahuano . . .
He went in and consulted Volume XLVI. Naturally,
he found not the slightest mention of Uqbar.

II

Some limited and waning memory of Herbert Ashe,
an engineer for the Southern Railway Line, still lin
gers in the hotel at Adrogué, among the effusive
honeysuckle vines and in the illusory depths of the
mirrors. In life, Ashe was afflicted with unreality, as

so many Englishmen are; in death, he is not even the ghost he was in life. He was tall and phlegmatic and his weary rectangular beard had once been red. I understand that he was a widower, and without issue. Every few years he would go back to England, to make his visit (I am judging from some photographs he showed us) to a sundial and a stand of oak trees. My father had forged one of those close English friendships with him (the first adjective is perhaps excessive) that begin by excluding confidences and soon eliminate conversation. They would exchange books and newspapers; they would wage taciturn battle at chess . . . I recall Ashe on the hotel veranda, holding a book of mathematics, looking up sometimes at the irrecoverable colors of the sky. One evening, we spoke about the duodecimal number system, in which twelve is written 10. Ashe said that by coincidence he was just then transposing some duodecimal table or other to sexagesimal (in which sixty is written 10). He added that he'd been commissioned to perform that task by a Norwegian man . . . in Rio Grande do Sul. Ashe and I had known each other for eight years, and he had never mentioned a stay in Brazil. We spoke of the bucolic rural life, of *capangas,* of the Brazilian etymology of the word 'gaucho' (which some older folk in Uruguay still pronounce as *ga-úcho*), and nothing more was said – God forgive me – of duodecimals. In September of 1937 (my family and I were no longer at the hotel), Herbert Ashe died of a ruptured aneurysm. A few days before his death, he had received a sealed, certified package from Brazil containing a book printed in octavo major. Ashe left it in the bar, where, months later, I found it. I began to leaf through it and suddenly I experienced a slight, astonished sense of dizziness that I shall not describe, since this is the story not of my emotions but of Uqbar and Tlön and Orbis Tertius. (On one particular Islamic night, which is called the Night of Nights, the secret portals of the heavens open wide and the water in the water jars is sweeter than on other nights; if those gates had opened as I sat there, I would not have felt what I was feeling that evening.) The book was written in English, and it consisted of 1001 pages. On the leather-bound volume's yellow spine I read these curious words, which were repeated on the false cover: *A First Encyclopædia of Tlön. Vol. XI. Hlaer to Jangr.* There was no date or place of publication. On the first page and again on the onionskin page that covered one of the color illustrations there was stamped a blue oval with this inscription: *Orbis Tertius*. Two years earlier, I had discovered in one of the volumes of a certain pirated encyclopedia a brief description of a false country; now fate had set before me something much more precious and painstaking. I now held in my hands a vast and systematic fragment of the entire history of an unknown planet, with its architectures and its playing cards, the horror of its mythologies and the murmur of its tongues, its emperors and its seas, its minerals and its birds and fishes, its algebra and its fire, its theological and metaphysical controversies – all joined, articulated, coherent, and with no visible doctrinal purpose or hint of parody.

In the 'Volume Eleven' of which I speak, there are allusions to later and earlier volumes. Néstor Ibarra, in a now-classic article in the *N.R.F.,* denied that such companion volumes exist; Ezequiel Martínez Estrada and Drieu La Rochelle have rebutted that doubt, perhaps victoriously. The fact is, the most diligent searches have so far proven futile. In vain have we ransacked the libraries of the two Americas and Europe. Alfonso Reyes, weary of those 'subordinate drudgeries of a detective nature,' has proposed that between us, we undertake to *reconstruct* the many massive volumes that are missing: *ex ungue leonem*. He figures, half-seriously, half in jest, that a generation of Tlönists would suffice. That bold estimate takes us back to the initial problem: Who, singular or plural, invented Tlön? The plural is, I suppose, inevitable, since the hypothesis of a single inventor – some infinite Leibniz working in obscurity and self-effacement – has been unanimously discarded. It is conjectured that this 'brave new world' is the work of a secret society of astronomers, biologists, engineers, metaphysicians, poets, chemists, algebrists, moralists, painters, geometers, . . . , guided and directed by some shadowy man of genius. There are many men adept in those diverse disciplines, but few capable of imagination – fewer still capable of subordinating imagination to a rigorous and systematic plan. The plan is so vast that the contribution of each writer is infinitesimal.

At first it was thought that Tlön was a mere chaos, an irresponsible act of imaginative license; today we know that it is a cosmos, and that the innermost laws that govern it have been formulated, however provisionally so. Let it suffice to remind the reader that the apparent contradictions of Volume Eleven are the foundation stone of the proof that the other volumes do in fact exist: the order that has been observed in it is just that lucid, just that fitting. Popular magazines have trumpeted, with pardonable excess, the zoology and topography of Tlön. In my view, its transparent tigers and towers of blood do not perhaps merit the constant attention of *all* mankind, but I might be so bold as to beg a few moments to outline its conception of the universe.

Hume declared for all time that while Berkeley's arguments admit not the slightest refutation, they inspire not the slightest conviction. That pronouncement is entirely true with respect to the earth, entirely false with respect to Tlön. The nations of that planet are, congenitally, idealistic. Their language and those things derived from their language – religion, literature, metaphysics – presuppose idealism. For the people of Tlön, the world is not an amalgam of *objects* in space; it is a heterogeneous series of independent *acts* – the world is successive, temporal, but not spatial. There are no nouns in the conjectural *Ursprache* of Tlön, from which its 'present-day' languages and dialects derive: there are impersonal verbs, modified by monosyllabic suffixes (or prefixes) functioning as adverbs. For example, there is no noun that corresponds to our word 'moon,' but there is a verb which in English would be 'to moonate' or 'to enmoon.' 'The moon rose above the river' is '*hlör u fang axaxaxas mlö,*' or, as Xul Solar succinctly translates: *Upward, behind the onstreaming it mooned.*

That principle applies to the languages of the southern hemisphere. In the northern hemisphere (about whose *Ursprache* Volume Eleven contains very little information), the primary unit is not the verb but the monosyllabic adjective. Nouns are formed by stringing together adjectives. One does not say 'moon'; one says 'aerial-bright above dark-round' or 'soft-amberish-celestial' or any other string. In this case, the complex of adjectives corresponds to a real object, but that is purely fortuitous. The literature of the northern hemisphere (as in Meinong's subsisting world) is filled with ideal objects, called forth and dissolved in an instant, as the poetry requires. Sometimes mere simultaneity creates them. There are things composed of two terms, one visual and the other auditory: the color of the rising sun and the distant caw of a bird. There are things composed of many: the sun and water against the swimmer's breast, the vague shimmering pink one sees when one's eyes are closed, the sensation of being swept along by a river and also by Morpheus. These objects of the second degree may be combined with others; the process, using certain abbreviations, is virtually infinite. There are famous poems composed of a single enormous word; this word is a 'poetic object' created by the poet. The fact that no one believes in the reality expressed by these nouns means, paradoxically, that there is no limit to their number. The languages of Tlön's northern hemisphere possess all the nouns of the Indo-European languages – and many, many more.

It is no exaggeration to say that the classical culture of Tlön is composed of a single discipline – psychology – to which all others are subordinate. I have said that the people of that planet conceive the universe as a series of mental processes that occur not in space but rather successively, in time. Spinoza endows his inexhaustible deity with the attributes of spatial extension and of thought; no one in Tlön would understand the juxtaposition of the first, which is typical only of certain states, and the second – which is a perfect synonym for the cosmos. Or to put it another way: space is not conceived as having duration in time. The perception of a cloud of smoke on the horizon and then the countryside on fire and then the half-extinguished cigarette that produced the scorched earth is considered an example of the association of ideas.

This thoroughgoing monism, or idealism, renders science null. To explain (or pass judgment on) an event is to link it to another; on Tlön, that joining-together is a posterior state of the *subject,* and can neither affect nor illuminate the prior state. Every mental state is irreducible: the simple act of giving it a name – i.e., of classifying it – introduces a distortion, a 'slant' or 'bias.' One might well deduce, therefore, that on Tlön there are no sciences – or even any 'systems of thought.' The paradoxical truth is that systems of thought do exist, almost countless numbers of them. Philosophies are much like the nouns of the northern hemisphere; the fact that every philosophy is by definition a dialectical game, a *Philosophie des Als Ob,* has allowed them to proliferate. There are systems upon systems that are incredible but possessed of a pleasing architecture or a certain agreeable sensationalism. The metaphysicians of Tlön seek not truth, or even plausibility – they seek to amaze, astound. In their view, metaphysics is a branch of the literature of fantasy. They know that a system is naught but the subordination of all the aspects of the universe to one of those aspects – *any* one of them. Even the phrase 'all the aspects' should be avoided, because it implies the impossible addition of the present instant and all those instants that went before. Nor is the plural 'those instants that went before' legitimate, for it implies another impossible operation . . . One of the schools of philosophy on Tlön goes so far as to deny the existence of time; it argues that the present is undefined and indefinite, the future has no reality except as present hope, and the past has no reality except as present recollection.* Another school posits that all time has already passed, so that our life is but the crepuscular memory, or crepuscular reflection, doubtlessly distorted

---

* Russell (*The Analysis of Mind* [1921], p. 159) posits that the world was created only moments ago, filled with human beings who 'remember' an illusory past.

and mutilated, of an irrecoverable process. Yet another claims that the history of the universe – and in it, our lives and every faintest detail of our lives – is the handwriting of a subordinate god trying to communicate with a demon. Another, that the universe might be compared to those cryptograms in which not all the symbols count, and only what happens every three hundred nights is actually real. Another, that while we sleep here, we are awake somewhere else, so that every man is in fact two men.

Of all the doctrines of Tlön, none has caused more uproar than materialism. Some thinkers have formulated this philosophy (generally with less clarity than zeal) as though putting forth a paradox. In order to make this inconceivable thesis more easily understood, an eleventh-century heresiarch* conceived the sophism of the nine copper coins, a paradox as scandalously famous on Tlön as the Eleatic aporiae to ourselves. There are many versions of that 'specious argument,' with varying numbers of coins and discoveries; the following is the most common:

* A 'century,' in keeping with the duodecimal system in use on Tlön, is a period of 144 years.

On Tuesday, X is walking along a deserted road and loses
nine copper coins. On Thursday, Y finds four coins in the
road, their luster somewhat dimmed by Wednesday's rain.
On Friday, Z discovers three coins in the road. Friday
morning X finds two coins on the veranda of his house.

From this story the heresiarch wished to deduce the
reality – i.e., the continuity in time – of those nine
recovered coins. 'It is absurd,' he said, 'to imagine
that four of the coins did not exist from Tuesday to
Thursday, three from Tuesday to Friday afternoon,
two from Tuesday to Friday morning. It is logical to
think that they in fact *did* exist – albeit in some secret
way that we are forbidden to understand – at every
moment of those three periods of time.'

The language of Tlön resisted formulating this
paradox; most people did not understand it. The
'common sense' school at first simply denied the
anecdote's veracity. They claimed it was a verbal fal-
lacy based on the reckless employment of two
neologisms, words unauthorized by standard usage
and foreign to all rigorous thought: the two verbs
'find' and 'lose,' which, since they presuppose the
identity of the nine first coins and the nine latter ones,

entail a *petitio principii*. These critics reminded their listeners that all nouns (*man, coin, Thursday, Wednesday, rain*) have only metaphoric value. They denounced the misleading detail that '[the coins'] luster [was] somewhat dimmed by Wednesday's rain' as presupposing what it attempted to prove: the continuing existence of the four coins from Tuesday to Thursday. They explained that 'equality' is one thing and 'identity' another, and they formulated a sort of *reductio ad absurdum* – the hypothetical case of nine men who on nine successive nights experience a sharp pain. Would it not be absurd, they asked, to pretend that the men had suffered one and the same pain?* They claimed that the heresiarch was motivated by the blasphemous desire to attribute the divine category *Being* to a handful of mere coins, and that he sometimes denied plurality and sometimes did not. They argued: If equality entailed identity, one would have to admit that the nine coins were a single coin.

---

* Today, one of Tlön's religions contends, platonically, that a certain pain, a certain greenish-yellow color, a certain temperature, and a certain sound are all the same, single reality. All men, in the dizzying instant of copulation, are the same man. All men who speak a line of Shakespeare *are* William Shakespeare.

Incredibly, those refutations did not put an end to the matter. A hundred years after the problem had first been posed, a thinker no less brilliant than the heresiarch, but of the orthodox tradition, formulated a most daring hypothesis. His happy conjecture was that there is but a single subject; that indivisible subject is every being in the universe, and the beings of the universe are the organs and masks of the deity. X is Y and is *also* Z. Z discovers three coins, then, because he remembers that X lost them; X finds two coins on the veranda of his house because he remembers that the others have been found ... Volume Eleven suggests that this idealistic pantheism triumphed over all other schools of thought for three primary reasons: first, because it repudiated solipsism; second, because it left intact the psychological foundation of the sciences; and third, because it preserved the possibility of religion. Schopenhauer (passionate yet lucid Schopenhauer) formulates a very similar doctrine in the first volume of his *Parerga und Paralipomean.*

Tlön's geometry is made up of two rather distinct disciplines – visual geometry and tactile geometry. Tactile geometry corresponds to our own, and is subordinate to the visual. Visual geometry is based on the surface, not the point; it has no parallel lines, and it claims that as one's body moves through space, it modifies the shapes that surround it. The basis of Tlön's arithmetic is the notion of indefinite numbers; it stresses the importance of the concepts 'greater than' and 'less than,' which our own mathematicians represent with the symbols > and <. The people of Tlön are taught that the act of counting modifies the amount counted, turning indefinites into definites. The fact that several persons counting the same quantity come to the same result is for the psychologists of Tlön an example of the association of ideas or of memorization. – We must always remember that on Tlön, the subject of knowledge is one and eternal.

Within the sphere of literature, too, the idea of the single subject is all-powerful. Books are rarely signed, nor does the concept of plagiarism exist: It has been decided that all books are the work of a single author who is timeless and anonymous. Literary criticism often invents authors: It will take two dissimilar works – the *Tao Te Ching* and the *1001 Nights,* for instance – attribute them to a single author, and then

n all good conscience determine the psychology of
that most interesting *homme de lettres* ...

Their books are also different from our own. Their
fiction has but a single plot, with every imaginable
permutation. Their works of a philosophical nature
invariably contain both the thesis and the antithesis,
the rigorous *pro* and *contra* of every argument. A book
that does not contain its counterbook is considered
incomplete.

Century upon century of idealism could hardly have
failed to influence reality. In the most ancient regions
of Tlön one may, not infrequently, observe the duplica-
tion of lost objects: Two persons are looking for a
pencil; the first person finds it, but says nothing; the
second finds a second pencil, no less real, but more in
keeping with his expectations. These secondary objects
are called *hrönir,* and they are, though awkwardly so,
slightly longer. Until recently, *hrönir* were the coincidental offspring of distraction and forgetfulness. It is
hard to believe that they have been systematically produced for only about a hundred years, but that is what
Volume Eleven tells us. The first attempts were unsuc-
cessful, but the *modus operandi* is worth recalling: The
warden of one of the state prisons informed his

prisoners that there were certain tombs in the ancient bed of a nearby river, and he promised that anyone who brought in an important find would be set free. For months before the excavation, the inmates were shown photographs of what they were going to discover. That first attempt proved that hope and greed can be inhibiting; after a week's work with pick and shovel, the only *hrön* unearthed was a rusty wheel, dated some time *later* than the date of the experiment. The experiment was kept secret, but was repeated afterward at four high schools. In three of them, the failure was virtually complete; in the fourth (where the principal happened to die during the early excavations), the students unearthed – or produced – a gold mask, an archaic sword, two or three clay amphorae, and the verdigris'd and mutilated torso of a king with an inscription on the chest that has yet to be deciphered. Thus it was discovered that no witnesses who were aware of the experimental nature of the search could be allowed near the site ... Group research projects produce conflicting finds; now individual, virtually spur-of-the-moment projects are preferred. The systematic production of *hrönir* (says Volume Eleven) has been of invaluable aid to archeaologists, making it possible not only to interrogate but even to modify the past, which is now no less plastic, no less malleable than the future. A curious bit of information: *hrönir* of the second and third remove – *hrönir* derived from another *hrön,* and *hrönir* derived from the *hrön* of a *hrön* – exaggerate the aberrations of the first; those of the fifth remove are almost identical; those of the ninth can be confused with those of the second; and those of the eleventh remove exhibit a purity of line that even the originals do not exhibit. The process is periodic: The *hrönir* of the twelfth remove begin to degenerate. Sometimes stranger and purer than any *hrön* is the *ur* – the thing produced by suggestion, the object brought forth by hope. The magnificent gold mask I mentioned is a distinguished example.

Things duplicate themselves on Tlön; they also tend to grow vague or 'sketchy,' and to lose detail when they begin to be forgotten. The classic example is the doorway that continued to exist so long as a certain beggar frequented it, but which was lost to sight when he died. Sometimes a few birds, a horse, have saved the ruins of an amphitheater.

Salto Oriental, 1940

POSTSCRIPT — 1947

I reproduce the article above exactly as it appeared in the *Anthology of Fantastic Literature* (1940), the only changes being editorial cuts of one or another metaphor and a tongue-in-cheek sort of summary that would now be considered flippant. So many things have happened since 1940 ... Allow me to recall some of them:

In March of 1941, a handwritten letter from Gunnar Erfjord was discovered in a book by Hinton that had belonged to Herbert Ashe. The envelope was postmarked Ouro Preto; the mystery of Tlön was fully elucidated by the letter. It confirmed Martínez Estrada's hypothesis: The splendid story had begun sometime in the early seventeenth century, one night in Lucerne or London. A secret benevolent society (which numbered among its members Dalgarno and, later, George Berkeley) was born; its mission: to invent a country. In its vague initial program, there figured 'hermetic studies,' philanthropy, and the Kabbalah. (The curious book by Valentinus Andreä dates from that early period.) After several years of confabulations and premature collaborative drafts, the members of the society realized that one generation would not suffice for creating and giving full expression to a country. They decided that each of the masters that belonged to the society would select a disciple to carry on the work. That hereditary arrangement was followed; after an interim of two hundred years, the persecuted fraternity turned up again in the New World. In 1824, in Memphis, Tennessee, one of the members had a conversation with the reclusive millionaire Ezra Buckley. Buckley, somewhat contemptuously, let the man talk – and then laughed at the modesty of the project. He told the man that in America it was nonsense to invent a country – what they ought to do was invent a planet. To that giant of an idea he added another, the brainchild of his nihilism*: The enormous enterprise must be kept secret. At that time the twenty volumes of the *Encyclopædia Britannica* were all the rage; Buckley suggested a systematic encyclopædia of the illusory planet. He would bequeath to them his gold-veined mountains, his navigable rivers, his prairies

---

* Buckley was a freethinker, a fatalist, and a defender of slavery.

thundering with bulls and buffalo, his Negroes, his brothels, and his dollars, he said, under one condition: 'The work shall make no pact with the impostor Jesus Christ.' Buckley did not believe in God, yet he wanted to prove to the nonexistent God that mortals could conceive and shape a world. Buckley was poisoned in Baton Rouge in 1828; in 1914 the society sent its members (now numbering three hundred) the final volume of the *First Encyclopædia of Tlön*. It was published secretly: the forty volumes that made up the work (the grandest work of letters ever undertaken by humankind) were to be the basis for another, yet more painstaking work, to be written this time not in English but in one of the languages of Tlön. That survey of an illusory world was tentatively titled *Orbis Tertius,* and one of its modest demiurges was Herbert Ashe – whether as agent or colleague of Gunnar Erfjord, I cannot say. His receipt of a copy of Volume Eleven seems to favor the second possibility. But what about the others? In 1942, the plot thickened. I recall with singular clarity one of the first events that occurred, something of whose premonitory nature I believe I sensed even then. It took place in an apartment on Laprida, across the street

rom a high, bright balcony that faced the setting
un. Princess Faucigny Lucinge had received from
Poitiers a crate containing her silver table service.
'rom the vast innards of a packing case emblazoned
vith international customs stamps she removed, one
by one, the fine unmoving things: plate from Utrecht
ind Paris chased with hard heraldic fauna, ... , a
amovar. Among the pieces, trembling softly but per-
:eptibly, like a sleeping bird, there throbbed,
nysteriously, a compass. The princess did not recog-
iize it. Its blue needle yearned toward magnetic
1orth; its metal casing was concave; the letters on its
lial belonged to one of the alphabets of Tlön. That
vas the first intrusion of the fantastic world of Tlön
nto the real world.

An unsettling coincidence made me a witness to
he second intrusion as well. This event took place
ome months later, in a sort of a country general-
tore-and-bar owned by a Brazilian man in the
Cuchilla Negra. Amorim and I were returning from
Sant'Anna. There was a freshet on the Tacuarembó;
1s there was no way to cross, we were forced to try
(to try to endure, that is) the rudimentary hospital-
ty at hand. The storekeeper set up some creaking

cots for us in a large storeroom clumsy with barrel and stacks of leather. We lay down, but we were kept awake until almost dawn by the drunkenness of an unseen neighbor, who swung between indecipherable streams of abuse and loudly sung snatches of *milongas* – or snatches of the same *milonga,* actually. As one can imagine, we attributed the man's insistent carrying-on to the storekeeper's fiery rotgut ... By shortly after daybreak, the man was dead in the hallway. The hoarseness of his voice had misled us – he was a young man. In his delirium, several coins had slipped from his wide gaucho belt, as had a gleaming metal cone about a die's width in diameter. A little boy tried to pick the cone-shaped object up, but in vain; a full-grown man could hardly do it. I held it for a few minutes in the palm of my hand; I recall that its weight was unbearable, and that even after someone took it from me, the sensation of terrible heaviness endured. I also recall the neat circle it engraved in my flesh. That evidence of a very small yet extremely heavy object left an unpleasant aftertaste of fear and revulsion. A *paisano* suggested that we throw it in the swollen river. Amorim purchased it for a few pesos

No one knew anything about the dead man, except that 'he came from the border.' Those small, incredibly heavy cones (made of a metal not of this world) are an image of the deity in certain Tlönian religions.

Here I end the personal portion of my narration. The rest lies in every reader's memory (if not his hope or fear). Let it suffice to recall, or mention, the subsequent events, with a simple brevity of words which the general public's concave memory will enrich or expand:

In 1944, an investigator from *The Nashville American* unearthed the forty volumes of *The First Encyclopædia of Tlön* in a Memphis library. To this day there is some disagreement as to whether that discovery was accidental or consented to and guided by the directors of the still-nebulous *Orbis Tertius;* the second supposition is entirely plausible. Some of the unbelievable features of Volume Eleven (the multiplication of *hrönir,* for example) have been eliminated or muted in the Memphis copy. It seems reasonable to suppose that the cuts obey the intent to set forth a world that is not *too* incompatible with the real world. The spread of Tlönian objects through various countries would complement that plan ... * At any rate, the international press made a great hue and cry about this 'find.' Handbooks, anthologies, surveys, 'literal translations,' authorized and pirated reprints of Mankind's Greatest Masterpiece filled the world, and still do. Almost immediately, reality 'caved in' at more than one point. The truth is, it wanted to cave in. Ten years ago, any symmetry, any system with an appearance of order – dialectical materialism, anti-Semitism, Nazism – could spellbind and hypnotize mankind. How could the world not fall under the sway of Tlön, how could it not yield to the vast and minutely detailed evidence of an ordered planet? It would be futile to reply that reality is also orderly. Perhaps it is, but orderly in accordance with divine laws (read: 'inhuman laws') that we can never quite manage to penetrate. Tlön may well be a labyrinth, but it is a labyrinth forged by men, a labyrinth destined to be deciphered by men.

Contact with Tlön, the *habit* of Tlön, has disintegrated this world. Spellbound by Tlön's rigor,

---

* There is still, of course, the problem of the *material* from which some objects are made.

humanity has forgotten, and continues to forget, that it is the rigor of chess masters, not of angels. Already Tlön's (conjectural) 'primitive language' has filtered into our schools; already the teaching of Tlön's harmonious history (filled with moving episodes) has obliterated the history that governed my own childhood; already a fictitious past has supplanted in men's memories that other past, of which we now know nothing certain – not even that it is false. Numismatics, pharmacology, and archeology have been reformed. I understand that biology and mathematics are also awaiting their next avatar ... A scattered dynasty of recluses has changed the face of the earth – and their work continues. If my projections are correct, a hundred years from now someone will discover the hundred volumes of *The Second Encyclopædia of Tlön*.

At that, French and English and mere Spanish will disappear from the earth. The world will be Tlön. That makes very little difference to me; through my quiet days in this hotel in Adrogué, I go on revising (though I never intend to publish) an indecisive translation in the style of Quevedo of Sir Thomas Browne's *Urne Buriall*.

The Book of Sand

. . . thy rope of sands . . . George Herbert (1593–1623)

The line consists of an infinite number of points; the plane, of an infinite number of lines; the volume, of an infinite number of planes; the hypervolume, of an infinite number of volumes . . . No – this, *more geometrico,* is decidedly not the best way to begin my tale. To say that the story is true is by now a convention of every fantastic tale; mine, nevertheless, *is* true.

I live alone, in a fifth-floor apartment on Calle Belgrano. One evening a few months ago, I heard a knock at my door. I opened it, and a stranger stepped in. He was a tall man, with blurred, vague features, or perhaps my nearsightedness made me see him that way. Everything about him spoke of honest poverty: he was dressed in gray, and carried a gray valise. I immediately sensed that he was a foreigner. At first I thought he was old; then I noticed that I had been misled by his sparse hair, which was blond, almost white, like the Scandinavians'. In the course of our conversation, which I doubt lasted more than an hour, I learned that he hailed from the Orkneys.

I pointed the man to a chair. He took some time to begin talking. He gave off an air of melancholy, as I myself do now.

'I sell Bibles,' he said at last.

'In this house,' I replied, not without a somewhat stiff, pedantic note, 'there are several English Bibles, including the first one, Wyclif's. I also have Cipriano de Valera's, Luther's (which is, in literary terms, the worst of the lot), and a Latin copy of the Vulgate. As you see, it isn't exactly Bibles I might be needing.'

After a brief silence he replied.

'It's not only Bibles I sell. I can show you a sacred book that might interest a man such as yourself. I came by it in northern India, in Bikaner.'

He opened his valise and brought out the book. He laid it on the table. It was a clothbound octavo volume that had clearly passed through many hands.

I examined it; the unusual heft of it surprised me. On the spine was printed *Holy Writ,* and then *Bombay.*

'Nineteenth century, I'd say,' I observed.

'I don't know,' was the reply. 'Never did know.'

I opened it at random. The characters were unfamiliar to me. The pages, which seemed worn and badly set, were printed in double columns, like a Bible. The text was cramped, and composed into versicles. At the upper corner of each page were Arabic numerals. I was struck by an odd fact: the even-numbered page would carry the number 40,514, let us say, while the odd-numbered page that followed it would be 999. I turned the page; the next page bore an eight-digit number. It also bore a small illustration, like those one sees in dictionaries: an anchor drawn in pen and ink, as though by the unskilled hand of a child.

It was at that point that the stranger spoke again.

'Look at it well. You will never see it again.'

There was a threat in the words, but not in the voice.

I took note of the page, and then closed the book. Immediately I opened it again. In vain I searched for the figure of the anchor, page after page. To hide my discomfiture, I tried another tack.

'This is a version of Scripture in some Hindu language, isn't that right?'

'No,' he replied.

Then he lowered his voice, as though entrusting me with a secret.

'I came across this book in a village on the plain, and I traded a few rupees and a Bible for it. The man who owned it didn't know how to read. I suspect he saw the Book of Books as an amulet. He was of the lowest caste; people could not so much as step on his shadow without being defiled. He told me his book was called the Book of Sand because neither sand nor this book has a beginning or an end.'

He suggested I try to find the first page.

I took the cover in my left hand and opened the book, my thumb and forefinger almost touching. It was impossible: several pages always lay between the cover and my hand. It was as though they grew from the very book.

'Now try to find the end.'

I failed there as well.

'This can't be,' I stammered, my voice hardly recognizable as my own.

'It can't be, yet it *is*,' The Bible peddler said, his voice little more than a whisper. 'The number of pages in this book is literally infinite. No page is the first page; no page is the last. I don't know why they're numbered in this arbitrary way, but perhaps it's to give one to understand that the terms of an infinite series can be numbered any way whatever.'

Then, as though thinking out loud, he went on.

'If space is infinite, we are anywhere, at any point in space. If time is infinite, we are at any point in time.'

His musings irritated me.

'You,' I said, 'are a religious man, are you not?'

'Yes, I'm Presbyterian. My conscience is clear. I am certain I didn't cheat that native when I gave him the Lord's Word in exchange for his diabolic book.'

I assured him he had nothing to reproach himself for, and asked whether he was just passing through the country. He replied that he planned to return to his own country within a few days. It was then that I learned he was a Scot, and that his home was in the Orkneys. I told him I had great personal fondness for Scotland because of my love for Stevenson and Hume.

'And Robbie Burns,' he corrected.

As we talked I continued to explore the infinite book.

'Had you intended to offer this curious specimen to the British Museum, then?' I asked with feigned indifference.

'No,' he replied, 'I am offering it to you,' and he mentioned a great sum of money.

I told him, with perfect honesty, that such an amount of money was not within my ability to pay. But my mind was working; in a few moments I had devised my plan.

'I propose a trade,' I said. 'You purchased the volume with a few rupees and the Holy Scripture; I will offer you the full sum of my pension, which I have just received, and Wyclif's black-letter Bible. It was left to me by my parents.'

'A black-letter Wyclif!' he murmured.

I went to my bedroom and brought back the money and the book. With a bibliophile's zeal he turned the pages and studied the binding.

'Done,' he said.

I was astonished that he did not haggle. Only later was I to realize that he had entered my house already determined to sell the book. He did not count the money, but merely put the bills into his pocket.

We chatted about India, the Orkneys, and the Norwegian jarls that had once ruled those islands. Night was falling when the man left. I have never seen him since, nor do I know his name.

I thought of putting the Book of Sand in the space left by the Wyclif, but I chose at last to hide it behind some imperfect volumes of the *Thousand and One Nights*.

I went to bed but could not sleep. At three or four in the morning I turned on the light. I took out the impossible book and turned its pages. On one, I saw an engraving of a mask. There was a number in the corner of the page – I don't remember now what it was – raised to the ninth power.

I showed no one my treasure. To the joy of possession was added the fear that it would be stolen from me, and to that, the suspicion that it might not be truly infinite. Those two points of anxiety aggravated my already habitual misanthropy. I had but few friends left, and those, I stopped seeing. A prisoner of the Book, I hardly left my house. I examined the worn binding and the covers with a magnifying glass, and rejected the possibility of some artifice. I found that the small illustrations were spaced at two-thousand-page intervals. I began noting them down in an alphabetized notebook, which was very soon filled. They never repeated themselves. At night, during the rare intervals spared me by insomnia, I dreamed of the book.

Summer was drawing to a close, and I realized that the book was monstrous. It was cold consolation to think that I, who looked upon it with my eyes and fondled it with my ten flesh-and-bone fingers, was no less monstrous than the book. I felt it was a nightmare thing, an obscene thing, and that it defiled and corrupted reality.

I considered fire, but I feared that the burning of an infinite book might be similarly infinite, and suffocate the planet in smoke.

I remembered reading once that the best place to hide a leaf is in the forest. Before my retirement I had worked in the National Library, which contained nine hundred thousand books; I knew that to the right of the lobby a curving staircase descended into the shadows of the basement, where the maps and periodicals are kept. I took advantage of the librarians' distraction to hide the Book of Sand on one of the library's damp shelves; I tried not to notice how high up, or how far from the door.

I now feel a little better, but I refuse even to walk down the street the library's on.

The Lottery in Babylon

Like all the men of Babylon, I have been proconsul;
like all, I have been a slave. I have known omnipotence, ignominy, imprisonment. Look here – my
right hand has no index finger. Look here – through
this gash in my cape you can see on my stomach a
crimson tattoo – it is the second letter, *Beth*. On
nights when the moon is full, this symbol gives me
power over men with the mark of Gimel, but it sub-
jects me to those with the Aleph, who on nights when
there is no moon owe obedience to those marked
with the Gimel. In the half-light of dawn, in a cellar,
standing before a black altar, I have slit the throats
of sacred bulls. Once, for an entire lunar year, I was
declared invisible – I would cry out and no one
would heed my call, I would steal bread and not be
beheaded. I have known that thing the Greeks knew
not – uncertainty. In a chamber of brass, as I faced

the strangler's silent scarf, hope did not abandon me; in the river of delights, panic has not failed me. Heraclides Ponticus reports, admiringly, that Pythagoras recalled having been Pyrrhus, and before that, Euphorbus, and before that, some other mortal; in order to recall similar vicissitudes, I have no need of death, nor even of imposture.

I owe that almost monstrous variety to an institution – the Lottery – which is unknown in other nations, or at work in them imperfectly or secretly. I have not delved into this institution's history. I know that sages cannot agree. About its mighty purposes I know as much as a man untutored in astrology might know about the moon. Mine is a dizzying country in which the Lottery is a major element of reality; until this day, I have thought as little about it as about the conduct of the indecipherable gods or of my heart. Now, far from Babylon and its beloved customs, I think with some bewilderment about the Lottery, and about the blasphemous conjectures that shrouded men whisper in the half-light of dawn or evening.

My father would tell how once, long ago – centuries? years? – the lottery in Babylon was a game played by commoners. He would tell (though whether this is true or not, I cannot say) how barbers would take a man's copper coins and give back rectangles made of bone or parchment and adorned with symbols. Then, in broad daylight, a drawing would be held; those smiled upon by fate would, with no further corroboration by chance, win coins minted of silver. The procedure, as you can see, was rudimentary.

Naturally, those so-called 'lotteries' were a failure. They had no moral force whatsoever; they appealed not to all a man's faculties, but only to his hopefulness. Public indifference soon meant that the merchants who had founded these venal lotteries began to lose money. Someone tried something new: including among the list of lucky numbers a few *unlucky* draws. This innovation meant that those who bought those numbered rectangles now had a twofold chance: they might win a sum of money or they might be required to pay a fine – sometimes a considerable one. As one might expect, that small risk (for every thirty 'good' numbers there was one ill-omened one) piqued the public's interest. Babylonians flocked to buy tickets. The man who bought none was considered a pusillanimous wretch, a man with no spirit of adventure. In time, this justified contempt found a second target:

not just the man who didn't play, but also the man who lost and paid the fine. The Company (as it was now beginning to be known) had to protect the interest of the winners, who could not be paid their prizes unless the pot contained almost the entire amount of the fines. A lawsuit was filed against the losers: the judge sentenced them to pay the original fine, plus court costs, or spend a number of days in jail. In order to thwart the Company, they all chose jail. From that gauntlet thrown down by a few men sprang the Company's omnipotence – its ecclesiastical, metaphysical force.

Some time after this, the announcements of the numbers drawn began to leave out the lists of fines and simply print the days of prison assigned to each losing number. That shorthand, as it were, which went virtually unnoticed at the time, was of utmost importance: *It was the first appearance of nonpecuniary elements in the lottery.* And it met with great success – indeed, the Company was forced by its players to increase the number of unlucky draws.

As everyone knows, the people of Babylon are great admirers of logic, and even of symmetry. It was inconsistent that lucky numbers should pay off in round silver coins while unlucky ones were measured in days and nights of jail. Certain moralists argued that the possession of coins did not always bring about happiness, and that other forms of happiness were perhaps more direct.

The lower-caste neighborhoods of the city voiced a different complaint. The members of the priestly class gambled heavily, and so enjoyed all the vicissitudes of terror and hope; the poor (with understandable, or inevitable, envy) saw themselves denied access to that famously delightful, even sensual, wheel. The fair and reasonable desire that all men and women, rich and poor, be able to take part equally in the Lottery inspired indignant demonstrations – the memory of which, time has failed to dim. Some stubborn souls could not (or pretended they could not) understand that this was a *novus ordo seclorum,* a necessary stage of history . . . A slave stole a crimson ticket; the drawing determined that that ticket entitled the bearer to have his tongue burned out. The code of law provided the same sentence for stealing a lottery ticket. Some Babylonians argued that the slave deserved the burning iron for being a thief; others, more magnanimous, that the executioner should employ the iron because thus fate had decreed . . . There were disturbances, there were regrettable instances of bloodshed, but the masses of Babylon at last, over the opposition of the well-to-do, imposed their will; they saw their generous objectives fully achieved. First, the Company was forced to assume all public power. (The unification was necessary because of the vastness and complexity of the new operations.) Second, the Lottery was made secret, free of charge, and open to all. The mercenary sale of lots was abolished; once initiated into the mysteries of Baal, every free citizen automatically took part in the sacred drawings, which were held in the labyrinths of the god every sixty nights and determined each citizen's destiny until the next drawing. The consequences were incalculable. A lucky draw might bring about a man's elevation to the council of the magi or the imprisonment of his enemy (secret, or known by all to be so), or might allow him to find, in the peaceful dimness of his room, the woman who would begin to disturb him, or whom he had never hoped to see again; an unlucky draw: mutilation, dishonor of many kinds, death itself. Sometimes a single event – the murder of C in a tavern, B's mysterious apotheosis – would be the inspired outcome of thirty or forty drawings. Combining bets was difficult, but we must recall that the individuals of the Company were (and still are) all-powerful, and clever. In many cases, the knowledge that certain happy turns were the simple result of chance would have lessened the force of those outcomes; to forestall that problem, agents of the Company employed suggestion, or even magic. The paths they followed, the intrigues they wove, were invariably secret. To penetrate the inner-most hopes and innermost fears of every man, they called upon astrologers and spies. There were certain stone lions, a sacred latrine called Qaphqa, some cracks in a dusty aqueduct – these places, it was generally believed, *gave access to the Company,* and well- or ill-wishing persons would deposit confidential reports in them. An alphabetical file held those *dossiers* of varying veracity.

Incredibly, there was talk of favoritism, of corruption. With its customary discretion, the Company did not reply directly; instead, it scrawled its brief argument in the rubble of a mask factory. This *apologia* is now numbered among the sacred Scriptures. It pointed out, doctrinally, that the Lottery is an interpolation of chance into the order of the universe, and observed that to accept errors is to strengthen chance, not contravene it. It also noted that those lions, that sacred squatting-place, though not disavowed by the Company (which reserved the right to consult them), functioned with no official guarantee.

This statement quieted the public's concerns. But it also produced other effects perhaps unforeseen by its author. It profoundly altered both the spirit and the operations of the Company. I have but little time remaining; we are told that the ship is about to sail – but I will try to explain.

However unlikely it may seem, no one, until that time, had attempted to produce a general theory of gaming. Babylonians are not a speculative people; they obey the dictates of chance, surrender their lives, their hopes, their nameless terror to it, but it never occurs to them to delve into its labyrinthine laws or the revolving spheres that manifest its workings. Nonetheless, the semiofficial statement that I mentioned inspired numerous debates of a legal and mathematical nature. From one of them, there emerged the following conjecture: If the Lottery is an intensification of chance, a periodic infusion of chaos into the cosmos, then is it not appropriate that chance intervene in *every* aspect of the drawing, not just one? Is it not ludicrous that chance should dictate a person's death while the circumstances of that death – whether private or public, whether drawn out for an hour or a century – should *not* be subject to chance? Those perfectly reasonable objections finally prompted sweeping reform; the complexities of the new system (complicated further by its having been in practice for centuries) are understood by only a handful of specialists, though I will attempt to summarize them, even if only symbolically.

Let us imagine a first drawing, which condemns an individual to death. In pursuance of that decree, another drawing is held; out of that second drawing come, say, nine possible executors. Of those nine, four might initiate a third drawing to determine the name of the executioner, two might replace the unlucky draw with a lucky one (the discovery of a treasure, say), another might decide that the death should be exacerbated (death with dishonor, that is, or with the refinement of torture), others might simply refuse to carry out the sentence . . . That is the scheme of the Lottery, put symbolically. *In reality, the number of drawings is infinite.* No decision is final; all branch into others. The ignorant assume that infinite drawings require infinite time; actually, all that is required is that time be infinitely subdivisible, as in the famous parable of the Race with the Tortoise. That infinitude coincides remarkably well with the sinuous numbers of Chance and with the Heavenly Archetype of the Lottery beloved of Platonists ... Some distorted echo of our custom seems to have reached the Tiber: In his *Life of Antoninus Heliogabalus,* Ælius Lampridius tells us that the emperor wrote out on seashells the fate that he intended for his guests at dinner – some would receive ten pounds of gold; others, ten houseflies, ten dormice, ten bears. It is fair to recall that Heliogabalus was raised in Asia Minor, among the priests of his eponymous god.

There are also *impersonal* drawings, whose purpose is unclear. One drawing decrees that a sapphire from Taprobana be thrown into the waters of the Euphrates; another, that a bird be released from the top of a certain tower; another, that every hundred years a grain of sand be added to (or taken from) the countless grains of sand on a certain beach. Sometimes, the consequences are terrible.

Under the Company's beneficent influence, our customs are now steeped in chance. The purchaser of a dozen amphoræ of Damascene wine will not be surprised if one contains a talisman, or a viper; the scribe who writes out a contract never fails to include some error; I myself, in this hurried statement, have misrepresented some splendor, some atrocity – perhaps, too, some mysterious monotony . . . Our historians, the most perspicacious on the planet, have invented a method for correcting chance; it is well known that the outcomes of this method are (in general) trustworthy – although, of course, they are never divulged without a measure of deception. Besides, there is nothing so tainted with fiction as the history of the Company . . . A paleographic document, unearthed at a certain temple, may come from yesterday's drawing or from a drawing that took place centuries ago. No book is published without some discrepancy between each of the edition's copies. Scribes take a secret oath to omit, interpolate, alter. *Indirect* falsehood is also practiced.

The Company, with godlike modesty, shuns all publicity. Its agents, of course, are secret; the orders it constantly (perhaps continually) imparts are no different from those spread wholesale by impostors. Besides – who will boast of being a mere impostor? The drunken man who blurts out an absurd command, the sleeping man who suddenly awakes and turns and chokes to death the woman sleeping at his side – are they not, perhaps, implementing one of the Company's secret decisions? That silent functioning, like God's, inspires all manner of conjectures. One scurrilously suggests that the Company ceased to exist hundreds of years ago, and that the sacred disorder of our lives is purely hereditary, traditional; another believes that the Company is eternal, and that it shall endure until the last night, when the last god shall annihilate the earth. Yet another declares that the Company is omnipotent, but affects only small things: the cry of a bird, the shades of rust and dust, the half dreams that come at dawn. Another, whispered by masked heresiarchs, says that *the Company has never existed, and never will*. Another, no less despicable, argues that it makes no difference whether one affirms or denies the reality of the shadowy corporation, because Babylon is nothing but an infinite game of chance.

Pierre Menard, Author of the Quixote

For Silvina Ocampo

The visible œuvre left by this novelist can be easily and briefly enumerated; unpardonable, therefore, are the omissions and additions perpetrated by Mme. Henri Bachelier in a deceitful catalog that a certain newspaper, whose Protestant leanings are surely no secret, has been so inconsiderate as to inflict upon that newspaper's deplorable readers – few and Calvinist (if not Masonic and circumcised) though they be. Menard's true friends have greeted that catalog with alarm, and even with a degree of sadness. One might note that only yesterday were we gathered before his marmoreal place of rest, among the dreary cypresses, and already Error is attempting to tarnish his bright Memory . . . Most decidedly, a brief rectification is imperative.

I am aware that it is easy enough to call my own scant authority into question. I hope, nonetheless, that I shall not be prohibited from mentioning two high testimonials. The baroness de Bacourt (at whose unforgettable *vendredis* I had the honor to meet the mourned-for poet) has been so kind as to approve the lines that follow. Likewise, the countess de Bagnoregio, one of the rarest and most cultured spirits of the principality of Monaco (now of Pittsburgh, Pennsylvania, following her recent marriage to the international philanthropist Simon Kautzsch – a man, it grieves me to say, vilified and slandered by the victims of his disinterested operations), has sacrificed 'to truth and to death' (as she herself has phrased it) the noble reserve that is the mark of her distinction, and in an open letter, published in the magazine *Luxe*, bestows upon me her blessing. Those commendations are sufficient, I should think.

I have said that the *visible* product of Menard's pen is easily enumerated. Having examined his personal files with the greatest care, I have established that his body of work consists of the following pieces:

a) a symbolist sonnet that appeared twice (with variants) in the review *La Conque* (in the numbers for March and October, 1899);

b) a monograph on the possibility of constructing a poetic vocabulary from concepts that are neither synonyms nor periphrastic locutions for the concepts that inform common speech, 'but are, rather, ideal objects created by convention essentially for the needs of poetry' (Nîmes, 1901);

c) a monograph on 'certain connections or affinities' between the philosophies of Descartes, Leibniz, and John Wilkins (Nîmes, 1903);

d) a monograph on Leibniz' *Characteristica universalis* (Nîmes, 1904);

e) a technical article on the possibility of enriching the game of chess by eliminating one of the rook's pawns (Menard proposes, recommends, debates, and finally rejects this innovation);

f) a monograph on Ramon Lull's *Ars magna generalis* (Nîmes, 1906);

g) a translation, with introduction and notes, of Ruy López de Segura's *Libro de la invención liberal y arte del juego del axedrez* (Paris, 1907);

h) drafts of a monograph on George Boole's symbolic logic;

i) a study of the essential metrical rules of French prose, illustrated with examples taken from Saint-Simon (*Revue des langues romanes*, Montpellier, October 1909);

j) a reply to Luc Durtain (who had countered that no such rules existed), illustrated with examples taken from Luc Durtain (*Revue des langues romanes,* Montpellier, December 1909);

k) a manuscript translation of Quevedo's *Aguja de navegar cultos,* titled *La boussole des précieux;*

l) a foreword to the catalog of an exhibit of lithographs by Carolus Hourcade (Nîmes, 1914);

m) a work entitled *Les problèmes d'un problème* (Paris, 1917), which discusses in chronological order the solutions to the famous problem of Achilles and the tortoise (two editions of this work have so far appeared; the second bears an epigraph consisting of Leibniz' advice *'Ne craignez point, monsieur, la tortue,'* and brings up to date the chapters devoted to Russell and Descartes);

n) a dogged analysis of the 'syntactical habits' of Toulet (*NRF,* March 1921) (Menard, I recall, affirmed that censure and praise were sentimental operations that bore not the slightest resemblance to criticism);

o) a transposition into alexandrines of Paul Valéry's *Cimetière marin* (*N.R.F.*, January 1928);

p) a diatribe against Paul Valéry, in Jacques Reboul's *Feuilles pour la suppression de la realité* (which diatribe, I might add parenthetically, states the exact reverse of Menard's true opinion of Valéry; Valéry understood this, and the two men's friendship was never imperiled);

q) a 'definition' of the countess de Bagnoregio, in the 'triumphant volume' (the phrase is that of another contributor, Gabriele d'Annunzio) published each year by that lady to rectify the inevitable biases of the popular press and to present 'to the world and all of Italy' a true picture of her person, which was so exposed (by reason of her beauty and her bearing) to erroneous and/or hasty interpretations;

r) a cycle of admirable sonnets dedicated to the baroness de Bacourt (1934);

s) a handwritten list of lines of poetry that owe their excellence to punctuation.*

This is the full extent (save for a few vague sonnets of occasion destined for Mme. Henri Bachelier's hospitable, or greedy, *album des souvenirs*) of the *visible* lifework of Pierre Menard, in proper chronological order. I shall turn now to the other, the subterranean, the interminably heroic production – the *œuvre non-pareil,* the *œuvre* that must remain – for such are our human limitations! – unfinished. This work, perhaps the most significant writing of our time, consists of the ninth and thirty-eighth chapters of Part I of *Don Quixote* and a fragment of Chapter XXII. I know that such a claim is on the face of it absurd; justifying that 'absurdity' shall be the primary object of this note.†

---

* Mme. Henri Bachelier also lists a literal translation of Quevedo's literal translation of St. Francis de Sales's *Introduction à la vie dévote.* In Pierre Menard's library there is no trace of such a work. This must be an instance of one of our friend's droll jokes, misheard or misunderstood.

† I did, I might say, have the secondary purpose of drawing a small sketch of the figure of Pierre Menard – but how dare I compete with the gilded pages I am told the baroness de Bacourt is even now preparing, or with the delicate sharp *crayon* of Carolus Hourcade?

Two texts, of distinctly unequal value, inspired the undertaking. One was that philological fragment by Novalis – number 2005 in the Dresden edition, to be precise – which outlines the notion of *total identification* with a given author. The other was one of those parasitic books that set Christ on a boulevard, Hamlet on La Cannebière, or don Quixote on Wall Street. Like every man of taste, Menard abominated those pointless travesties, which, Menard would say, were good for nothing but occasioning a plebeian delight in anachronism or (worse yet) captivating us with the elementary notion that all times and places are the same, or are different. It might be more interesting, he thought, though of contradictory and superficial execution, to attempt what Daudet had so famously suggested: conjoin in a single figure (Tartarin, say) both the Ingenious Gentleman don Quixote and his squire . . .

Those who have insinuated that Menard devoted his life to writing a contemporary *Quixote* besmirch his illustrious memory. Pierre Menard did not want to compose *another* Quixote, which surely is easy enough – he wanted to compose *the* Quixote. Nor, surely, need one be obliged to note that his goal was never a mechanical transcription of the original; he had no intention of *copying* it. His admirable ambition was to produce a number of pages which coincided – word for word and line for line – with those of Miguel de Cervantes.

'My purpose is merely astonishing,' he wrote me on September 30, 1934, from Bayonne. 'The final term of a theological or metaphysical proof – the world around us, or God, or chance, or universal Forms – is no more final, no more uncommon, than my revealed novel. The sole difference is that philosophers publish pleasant volumes containing the intermediate stages of their work, while I am resolved to suppress those stages of my own.' And indeed there is not a single draft to bear witness to that years-long labor.

Initially, Menard's method was to be relatively simple: Learn Spanish, return to Catholicism, fight against the Moor or Turk, forget the history of Europe from 1602 to 1918 – *be* Miguel de Cervantes. Pierre Menard weighed that course (I know he pretty thoroughly mastered seventeenth-century Castilian) but he discarded it as too easy. Too impossible, rather!, the reader will say. Quite so, but the undertaking was impossible from the outset, and of all the impossible ways of bringing it about, this was the least interesting. To be a popular novelist of the seventeenth century in the twentieth seemed to Menard to be a diminution. Being, somehow, Cervantes, and arriving thereby at the Quixote – that looked to Menard less challenging (and therefore less interesting) than continuing to be Pierre Menard and coming to the Quixote *through the experiences of Pierre Menard.* (It was that conviction, by the way, that obliged him to leave out the autobiographical foreword to Part II of the novel. Including the prologue would have meant creating another character – 'Cervantes' – and also presenting Quixote through that character's eyes, not Pierre Menard's. Menard, of course, spurned that easy solution.) 'The task I have undertaken is not *in essence* difficult,' I read at another place in that letter. 'If I could just be immortal, I could do it.' Shall I confess that I often imagine that he did complete it, and that I read the Quixote – the *entire* Quixote – as if Menard had conceived it? A few nights ago, as I was leafing through Chapter XXVI (never attempted by Menard), I recognized our friend's style, could almost hear his voice in this marvelous phrase: 'the nymphs of the rivers, the moist and grieving Echo.'

That wonderfully effective linking of one adjective of emotion with another of physical description brought to my mind a line from Shakespeare, which I recall we discussed one afternoon:

Where a malignant and a turban'd Turk . . .

Why the Quixote? my reader may ask. That choice, made by a Spaniard, would not have been incomprehensible, but it no doubt is so when made by a *Symboliste* from Nîmes, a devotee essentially of Poe – who begat Baudelaire, who begat Mallarmé, who begat Valéry, who begat M. Edmond Teste. The letter mentioned above throws some light on this point. 'The *Quixote*,' explains Menard,

deeply interests me, but does not seem to me – comment dirai-je? *– inevitable. I cannot imagine the universe without Poe's ejaculation 'Ah, bear in mind this garden was enchanted!' or the* Bateau ivre *or the* Ancient Mariner, *but I know myself able to imagine it without the* Quixote. *(I am speaking, of course, of my personal ability, not of the historical resonance of those works.) The* Quixote *is a contingent work; the* Quixote *is not necessary. I can premeditate committing it to writing, as it were – I can write* *it – without falling into a tautology. At the age of twelve or thirteen I read it – perhaps read it cover to cover, I cannot recall. Since then, I have carefully reread certain chapters, those which, at least for the moment, I shall not attempt. I have also glanced at the interludes, the comedies, the* Galatea, *the Exemplary Novels, the undoubtedly laborious* Travails of Persiles and Sigismunda, *and the poetic* Voyage to Parnassus . . . *My general recollection of the* Quixote, *simplified by forgetfulness and indifference, might well be the equivalent of the vague foreshadowing of a yet unwritten book. Given that image (which no one can in good conscience deny me), my problem is, without the shadow of a doubt, much more difficult than Cervantes'. My obliging predecessor did not spurn the collaboration of chance; his method of composition for the immortal book was a bit* à la diable, *and he was often swept along by the inertiæ of the language and the imagination. I have assumed the mysterious obligation to reconstruct, word for word, the novel that for him was spontaneous. This game of solitaire I play is governed by two polar rules: the first allows me to try out formal or psychological variants; the second forces me to sacrifice them to the 'original' text and to come, by irrefutable arguments, to those eradications . . . In addition to these first two artificial constraints there is another, inherent to the project. Composing the* Quixote *in the early seventeenth century was a reasonable, necessary, perhaps even inevitable undertaking; in the early twentieth, it is virtually impossible. Not for nothing have three hundred years elapsed, freighted with the most complex events. Among those events, to mention but one, is the* Quixote *itself.*

In spite of those three obstacles, Menard's fragmentary Quixote is more subtle than Cervantes'. Cervantes crudely juxtaposes the humble provincial reality of his country against the fantasies of the romance, while Menard chooses as his 'reality' the land of Carmen during the century that saw the Battle of Lepanto and the plays of Lope de Vega. What burlesque brushstrokes of local color that choice would have inspired in a Maurice Barrès or a Rodríguez Larreta! Yet Menard, with perfect naturalness, avoids them. In his work, there are no gypsy goings-on or conquistadors or mystics or Philip IIs or *autos da fé*. He ignores, overlooks – or banishes – local color. That disdain posits a new meaning for the 'historical novel.' That disdain condemns *Salammbô,* with no possibility of appeal.

No less amazement visits one when the chapters are considered in isolation. As an example, let us look at Part I, Chapter XXXVIII, 'which treats of the curious discourse that Don Quixote made on the subject of arms and letters.' It is a matter of common knowledge that in that chapter, don Quixote (like Quevedo in the analogous, and later, passage in *La hora de todos*) comes down against letters and in favor of arms. Cervantes was an old soldier; from him, the verdict is understandable. But that *Pierre Menard*'s don Quixote – a contemporary of *La trahison des clercs* and Bertrand Russell – should repeat those cloudy sophistries! Mme. Bachelier sees in them an admirable (typical) subordination of the author to the psychology of the hero; others (lacking all perspicacity) see them as a *transcription* of the Quixote; the baroness de Bacourt, as influenced by Nietzsche. To that third interpretation (which I consider irrefutable), I am not certain I dare to add a fourth, though it agrees very well with the almost divine modesty of Pierre Menard: his resigned or ironic habit of putting forth ideas that were the exact opposite of those he actually held. (We should recall that diatribe against Paul Valéry in the ephemeral Surrealist journal edited by Jacques Reboul.) The Cervantes text and the Menard text are verbally identical, but the second is almost infinitely richer. (More *ambiguous,* his detractors will say – but ambiguity is richness.)

It is a revelation to compare the *Don Quixote* of Pierre Menard with that of Miguel de Cervantes. Cervantes, for example, wrote the following (Part I, Chapter IX):

. . . truth, whose mother is history, rival of time, depository of deeds, witness of the past, exemplar and adviser to the present, and the future's counselor.

This catalog of attributes, written in the seventeenth century, and written by the 'ingenious layman' Miguel de Cervantes, is mere rhetorical praise of history. Menard, on the other hand, writes:

. . . truth, whose mother is history, rival of time, depository of deeds, witness of the past, exemplar and adviser to the present, and the future's counselor.

History, the *mother* of truth! – the idea is staggering. Menard, a contemporary of William James, defines history not as a *delving into* reality but as the very *fount* of reality. Historical truth, for Menard, is not 'what happened'; it is what we *believe* happened. The final phrases – *exemplar and adviser to the present, and the future's counselor* – are brazenly pragmatic.

The contrast in styles is equally striking. The archaic style of Menard – who is, in addition, not a native speaker of the language in which he writes – is somewhat affected. Not so the style of his precursor, who employs the Spanish of his time with complete naturalness.

There is no intellectual exercise that is not ultimately pointless. A philosophical doctrine is, at first, a plausible description of the universe; the years go by, and it is a mere chapter – if not a paragraph or proper noun – in the history of philosophy. In literature, that 'falling by the wayside,' that loss of 'relevance,' is even better known. The Quixote, Menard remarked, was first and foremost a pleasant book; it is now an occasion for patriotic toasts, grammatical arrogance, obscene *de luxe* editions. Fame is a form – perhaps the worst form – of incomprehension.

Those nihilistic observations were not new; what was remarkable was the decision that Pierre Menard derived from them. He resolved to anticipate the vanity that awaits all the labors of mankind; he undertook a task of infinite complexity, a task futile from the outset. He dedicated his scruples and his nights 'lit by midnight oil' to repeating in a foreign tongue a book that already existed. His drafts were endless; he stubbornly corrected, and he ripped up thousands of handwritten pages. He would allow no one to see them, and took care that they not survive him.* In vain have I attempted to reconstruct them.

I have reflected that it is legitimate to see the 'final' Quixote as a kind of palimpsest, in which the traces – faint but not undecipherable – of our friend's 'previous' text must shine through. Unfortunately, only a second Pierre Menard, reversing the labors of the first, would be able to exhume and revive those Troys . . .

'Thinking, meditating, imagining,' he also wrote me, 'are not anomalous acts – they are the normal

---

* I recall his square-ruled notebooks, his black crossings-out, his peculiar typographical symbols, and his insect-like handwriting. In the evening, he liked to go out for walks on the outskirts of Nîmes; he would often carry along a notebook and make a cheery bonfire.

respiration of the intelligence. To glorify the occasional exercise of that function, to treasure beyond price ancient and foreign thoughts, to recall with incredulous awe what some *doctor universalis* thought, is to confess our own languor, or our own *barbarie.* Every man should be capable of all ideas, and I believe that in the future he shall be.'

Menard has (perhaps unwittingly) enriched the slow and rudimentary art of reading by means of a new technique – the technique of deliberate anachronism and fallacious attribution. That technique, requiring infinite patience and concentration, encourages us to read the *Odyssey* as though it came after the *Æneid,* to read Mme. Henri Bachelier's *Le jardin du Centaure* as though it were written by Mme. Henri Bachelier. This technique fills the calmest books with adventure. Attributing the *Imitatio Christi* to Louis Ferdinand Céline or James Joyce – is that not sufficient renovation of those faint spiritual admonitions?

Nîmes, 1939

The Circular Ruins

And if he left off dreaming about you . . .
Through the Looking-Glass, *VI*

No one saw him slip from the boat in the unanimous night, no one saw the bamboo canoe as it sank into the sacred mud, and yet within days there was no one who did not know that the taciturn man had come there from the South, and that his homeland was one of those infinite villages that lie upriver, on the violent flank of the mountain, where the language of the Zend is uncontaminated by Greek and where leprosy is uncommon. But in fact the gray man had kissed the mud, scrambled up the steep bank (without pushing back, probably without even feeling, the sharp-leaved bulrushes that slashed his flesh), and dragged himself, faint and bloody, to the circular enclosure, crowned by the stone figure of a horse or tiger, which had once been the color of fire but was now the color of ashes. That ring was a temple devoured by an ancient holocaust; now, the malarial jungle had profaned it and its god went unhonored by mankind. The foreigner lay down at the foot of the pedestal.

He was awakened by the sun high in the sky. He examined his wounds and saw, without astonishment, that they had healed; he closed his pale eyes and slept, not out of any weakness of the flesh but out of willed determination. He knew that this temple was the place that his unconquerable plan called for; he knew that the unrelenting trees had not succeeded in strangling the ruins of another promising temple downriver – like this one, a temple to dead, incinerated gods; he knew that his immediate obligation was to sleep. About midnight he was awakened by the inconsolable cry of a bird. Prints of unshod feet, a few figs, and a jug of water told him that the men of the region had respectfully spied upon his sleep and that they sought his favor, or feared his magic. He felt the coldness of fear, and he sought out a tomblike niche in the crumbling wall, where he covered himself with unknown leaves.

The goal that led him on was not impossible, though it was clearly supernatural: He wanted to dream a man. He wanted to dream him completely, in painstaking detail, and impose him upon reality. This magical objective had come to fill his entire soul; if someone had asked him his own name, or inquired into any feature of his life till then, he would not have been able to answer. The uninhabited and crumbling temple suited him, for it was a minimum of visible world; so did the proximity of the woodcutters, for they saw to his frugal needs. The rice and fruit of their tribute were nourishment enough for his body, which was consecrated to the sole task of sleeping and dreaming.

At first, his dreams were chaotic; a little later, they became dialectical. The foreigner dreamed that he was in the center of a circular amphitheater, which was somehow the ruined temple; clouds of taciturn students completely filled the terraces of seats. The faces of those farthest away hung at many centuries' distance and at a cosmic height, yet they were absolutely clear. The man lectured on anatomy, cosmography, magic; the faces listened earnestly, intently, and attempted to respond with understanding – as though they sensed the importance of that education that would redeem one of them from his state of hollow appearance and insert him into the real world. The man, both in sleep and when awake, pondered his phantasms' answers; he did not allow himself to be taken in by impostors, and he sensed in certain perplexities a growing intelligence. He was seeking a soul worthy of taking its place in the universe.

On the ninth or tenth night, he realized (with some bitterness) that nothing could be expected from those students who passively accepted his teachings, but only from those who might occasionally, in a reasonable way, venture an objection. The first – the accepting – though worthy of affection and a degree of sympathy, would never emerge as individuals; the latter – those who sometimes questioned – had a bit more preexistence. One afternoon (afternoons now paid their tribute to sleep as well; now the man was awake no more than two or three hours around daybreak) he dismissed the vast illusory classroom once and for all and retained but a single pupil – a taciturn, sallow-skinned young man, at times intractable, with sharp features that echoed those of the man that dreamed him. The pupil was not disconcerted for long by the elimination of his classmates; after only a few of the private classes, his progress amazed his teacher. Yet disaster would not be forestalled. One day the man emerged from sleep as though from a viscous desert, looked up at the hollow light of the evening (which for a moment he confused with the light of dawn), and realized that he had not dreamed. All that night and the next day, the unbearable lucidity of insomnia harried him, like a hawk. He went off to explore the jungle, hoping to tire himself; among the hemlocks he managed no more than a few intervals of feeble sleep, fleetingly veined with the most rudimentary of visions – useless to him. He reconvened his class, but no sooner had he spoken a few brief words of exhortation than the faces blurred, twisted, and faded away. In his almost perpetual state of wakefulness, tears of anger burned the man's old eyes.

He understood that the task of molding the incoherent and dizzying stuff that dreams are made of is the most difficult work a man can undertake, even if he fathom all the enigmas of the higher and lower spheres – much more difficult than weaving a rope of sand or minting coins of the faceless wind. He understood that initial failure was inevitable. He swore to put behind him the vast hallucination that at first had drawn him off the track, and he sought another way to approach his task. Before he began, he devoted a month to recovering the strength his delirium had squandered. He abandoned all premeditation of dreaming, and almost instantly managed to sleep for a fair portion of the day. The few times he did dream during this period, he did not focus on his dreams; he would wait to take up his task again until the disk of the moon was whole. Then, that evening, he purified himself in the waters of the river, bowed down to the planetary gods, uttered those syllables of a powerful name that it is lawful to pronounce, and laid himself down to sleep. Almost immediately he dreamed a beating heart.

He dreamed the heart warm, active, secret – about the size of a closed fist, a garnet-colored thing inside the dimness of a human body that was still faceless and sexless; he dreamed it, with painstaking love, for fourteen brilliant nights. Each night he perceived it with greater clarity, greater certainty. He did not touch it; he only witnessed it, observed it, corrected it, perhaps, with his eyes. He perceived it, he *lived* it, from many angles, many distances. On the fourteenth night, he stroked the pulmonary artery with his forefinger, and then the entire heart, inside and out. And his inspection made him proud. He deliberately did not sleep the next night; then he took up the heart again, invoked the name of a planet, and set about dreaming another of the major organs. Before the year was out he had reached the skeleton, the eyelids. The countless hairs of the body were perhaps the most difficult task. The man had dreamed a fully fleshed man – a stripling – but this youth did not stand up or speak, nor could it open its eyes. Night after night, the man dreamed the youth asleep.

In the cosmogonies of the Gnostics, the demiurges knead up a red Adam who cannot manage to stand; as rude and inept and elementary as that Adam of dust was the Adam of dream wrought from the sorcerer's nights. One afternoon, the man almost destroyed his creation, but he could not bring himself to do it. (He'd have been better off if he had.) After making vows to all the deities of the earth and the river, he threw himself at the feet of the idol that was perhaps a tiger or perhaps a colt, and he begged for its untried aid. That evening, at sunset, the statue filled his dreams. In the dream it was alive, and trembling – yet it was not the dread-inspiring hybrid form of horse and tiger it had been. It was, instead, those two vehement creatures plus bull, and rose, and tempest, too – and all that, simultaneously. The manifold god revealed to the man that its earthly name was Fire, and that in that circular temple (and others like it) men had made sacrifices and worshiped it, and that it would magically bring to life the phantasm the man had dreamed – so fully bring him to life that every creature, save Fire itself and the man who dreamed him, would take him for a man of flesh and blood. Fire ordered the dreamer to send the youth, once instructed in the rites, to that other ruined temple whose pyramids still stood downriver, so that a voice might glorify the god in that deserted place. In the dreaming man's dream, the dreamed man awoke.

The sorcerer carried out Fire's instructions. He consecrated a period of time (which in the end encompassed two full years) to revealing to the youth the arcana of the universe and the secrets of the cult of Fire. Deep inside, it grieved the man to separate himself from his creation. Under the pretext of pedagogical necessity, he drew out the hours of sleep more every day. He also redid the right shoulder (which was perhaps defective). From time to time, he was disturbed by a sense that all this had happened before . . . His days were, in general, happy; when he closed his eyes, he would think *Now I will be with my son*. Or, less frequently, *The son I have engendered is waiting for me, and he will not exist if I do not go to him*.

Gradually, the man accustomed the youth to reality. Once he ordered him to set a flag on a distant mountaintop. The next day, the flag crackled on the summit. He attempted other, similar experiments – each more daring than the last. He saw with some bitterness that his son was ready – perhaps even impatient – to be born. That night he kissed him for the first time, then sent him off, through many leagues of impenetrable jungle, many leagues of swamp, to that other temple whose ruins bleached in the sun downstream. But first (so that the son would never know that he was a phantasm, so that he would believe himself to be a man like other men) the man infused in him a total lack of memory of his years of education.

The man's victory, and his peace, were dulled by

the wearisome sameness of his days. In the twilight hours of dusk and dawn, he would prostrate himself before the stone figure, imagining perhaps that his unreal son performed identical rituals in other circular ruins, downstream. At night he did not dream, or dreamed the dreams that all men dream. His perceptions of the universe's sounds and shapes were somewhat pale: the absent son was nourished by those diminutions of his soul. His life's goal had been accomplished; the man lived on now in a sort of ecstasy. After a period of time (which some tellers of the story choose to compute in years, others in decades), two rowers woke the man at midnight. He could not see their faces, but they told him of a magical man in a temple in the North, a man who could walk on fire and not be burned.

The sorcerer suddenly remembered the god's words. He remembered that of all the creatures on the earth, Fire was the only one who knew that his son was a phantasm. That recollection, comforting at first, soon came to torment him. He feared that his son would meditate upon his unnatural privilege and somehow discover that he was a mere simulacrum. To be not a man, but the projection of another man's dream – what incomparable humiliation, what vertigo! Every parent feels concern for the children he has procreated (or allowed to be procreated) in happiness or in mere confusion; it was only natural that the sorcerer should fear for the future of the son he had conceived organ by organ, feature by feature, through a thousand and one secret nights.

The end of his meditations came suddenly, but it had been foretold by certain signs: first (after a long drought), a distant cloud, as light as a bird, upon a mountaintop; then, toward the South, the sky the pinkish color of a leopard's gums; then the clouds of smoke that rusted the iron of the nights; then, at last, the panicked flight of the animals – for that which had occurred hundreds of years ago was being repeated now. The ruins of the sanctuary of the god of Fire were destroyed by fire. In the birdless dawn, the sorcerer watched the concentric holocaust close in upon the walls. For a moment he thought of taking refuge in the water, but then he realized that death would be a crown upon his age and absolve him from his labors. He walked into the tatters of flame, but they did not bite his flesh – they caressed him, bathed him without heat and without combustion. With relief, with humiliation, with terror, he realized that he, too, was but appearance, that another man was dreaming him.

Shakespeare's Memory

There are devotees of Goethe, of the Eddas, of the late song of the Nibelungen; my fate has been Shakespeare. As it still is, though in a way that no one could have foreseen – no one save one man, Daniel Thorpe, who has just recently died in Pretoria. There is another man, too, whose face I have never seen.

My name is Hermann Sörgel. The curious reader may have chanced to leaf through my *Shakespeare Chronology,* which I once considered essential to a proper understanding of the text: it was translated into several languages, including Spanish. Nor is it beyond the realm of possibility that the reader will recall a protracted diatribe against an emendation inserted by Theobald into his critical edition of 1734 – an emendation which became from that moment on an unquestioned part of the canon. Today I am taken a bit aback by the uncivil tone of those pages, which

I might almost say were written by another man. In 1914 I drafted, but did not publish, an article on the compound words that the Hellenist and dramatist George Chapman coined for his versions of Homer; in forging these terms, Chapman did not realize that he had carried English back to its Anglo-Saxon origins, the *Ursprung* of the language. It never occurred to me that Chapman's voice, which I have now forgotten, might one day be so familiar to me . . . A scattering of critical and philological 'notes,' as they are called, signed with my initials, complete, I believe, my literary biography. Although perhaps I might also be permitted to include an unpublished translation of *Macbeth,* which I began in order to distract my mind from the thought of the death of my brother, Otto Julius, who fell on the western front in 1917. I never finished translating the play; I came to realize that English has (to its credit) two registers – the Germanic and the Latinate – while our own German, in spite of its greater musicality, must content itself with one.

I mentioned Daniel Thorpe. I was introduced to Thorpe by Major Barclay at a Shakespeare conference. I will not say where or when; I know all too well that such specifics are in fact vaguenesses.

More important than Daniel Thorpe's face, which my partial blindness helps me to forget, was his notorious lucklessness. When a man reaches a certain age, there are many things he can feign; happiness is not one of them. Daniel Thorpe gave off an almost physical air of melancholy.

After a long session, night found us in a pub – an undistinguished place that might have been any pub in London. To make ourselves feel that we were in England (which of course we were), we drained many a ritual pewter mug of dark warm beer.

'In Punjab,' said the major in the course of our conversation, 'a fellow once pointed out a beggar to me. Islamic legend apparently has it, you know, that King Solomon owned a ring that allowed him to understand the language of the birds. And this beggar, so everyone believed, had somehow come into possession of that ring. The value of the thing was so beyond all reckoning that the poor bugger could never sell it, and he died in one of the courtyards of the mosque of Wazil Khan, in Lahore.'

It occurred to me that Chaucer must have been familiar with the tale of that miraculous ring, but mentioning it would have spoiled Barclay's anecdote.

'And what became of the ring?' I asked.

'Lost now, of course, as that sort of magical thinga-majig always is. Probably in some secret hiding place in the mosque, or on the finger of some chap who's off living somewhere where there're no birds.'

'Or where there are so many,' I noted, 'that one can't make out what they're saying for the racket. Your story has something of the parable about it, Barclay.'

It was at that point that Daniel Thorpe spoke up. He spoke, somehow, impersonally, without looking at us. His English had a peculiar accent, which I attributed to a long stay in the East.

'It is not a parable,' he said. 'Or if it is, it is none-theless a true story. There are things that have a price so high they can never be sold.'

The words I am attempting to reconstruct impressed me less than the conviction with which Daniel Thorpe spoke them. We thought he was going to say something further, but suddenly he fell mute, as though he regretted having spoken at all. Barclay said good night. Thorpe and I returned together to the hotel. It was quite late by now, but Thorpe suggested we continue our conversation in his room. After a short exchange of trivialities, he said to me:

'Would you like to own King Solomon's ring? I offer it to you. That's a metaphor, of course, but the thing the metaphor stands for is every bit as wondrous as that ring. Shakespeare's memory, from his youngest boyhood days to early April, 1616 – I offer it to you.'

I could not get a single word out. It was as though I had been offered the ocean.

Thorpe went on:

'I am not an impostor. I am not insane. I beg you to suspend judgment until you hear me out. Major Barclay no doubt told you that I am, or was, a military physician. The story can be told very briefly. It begins in the East, in a field hospital, at dawn. The exact date is not important. An enlisted man named Adam Clay, who had been shot twice, offered me the precious memory almost literally with his last breath. Pain and fever, as you know, make us creative; I accepted his offer without crediting it – and besides, after a battle, nothing seems so very strange. He barely had time to explain the singular conditions of the gift: The one who possesses it must offer it aloud, and the one who is to receive it must accept it the same way. The man who gives it loses it forever.'

The name of the soldier and the pathetic scene of the bestowal struck me as 'literary' in the worst sense of the word. It all made me a bit leery.

'And you, now, possess Shakespeare's memory?'

'What I possess,' Thorpe answered, 'are still *two* memories – my own personal memory and the memory of that Shakespeare that I partially am. Or rather, two memories possess *me*. There is a place where they merge, somehow. There is a woman's face . . . I am not sure what century it belongs to.'

'And the one that was Shakespeare's –' I asked. 'What have you done with it?'

There was silence.

'I have written a fictionalized biography,' he then said at last, 'which garnered the contempt of critics but won some small commercial success in the United States and the colonies. I believe that's all . . . I have warned you that my gift is not a sinecure. I am still waiting for your answer.'

I sat thinking. Had I not spent a lifetime, colorless yet strange, in pursuit of Shakespeare? Was it not fair that at the end of my labors I find him?

I said, carefully pronouncing each word:

'I accept Shakespeare's memory.'

Something happened; there is no doubt of that. But I did not feel it happen.

Perhaps just a slight sense of fatigue, perhaps imaginary.

I clearly recall that Thorpe did tell me:

'The memory has entered your mind, but it must be "discovered." It will emerge in dreams or when you are awake, when you turn the pages of a book or turn a corner. Don't be impatient; don't *invent* recollections. Chance in its mysterious workings may help it along, or it may hold it back. As I gradually forget, you will remember. I can't tell you how long the process will take.'

We dedicated what remained of the night to a discussion of the character of Shylock. I refrained from trying to discover whether Shakespeare had had personal dealings with Jews. I did not want Thorpe to imagine that I was putting him to some sort of test. I did discover (whether with relief or uneasiness, I cannot say) that his opinions were as academic and conventional as my own.

In spite of that long night without sleep, I hardly slept at all the following night. I found, as I had so many times before, that I was a coward. Out of fear of disappointment, I could not deliver myself up to openhanded hope. I preferred to think that Thorpe's gift was illusory. But hope did, irresistibly, come to prevail. I would possess Shakespeare, and possess him as no one had ever possessed anyone before – not in love, or friendship, or even hatred. I, in some way, would *be* Shakespeare. Not that I would write the tragedies or the intricate sonnets – but I would recall the instant at which the witches (who are also the Fates) had been revealed to me, the other instant at which I had been given the vast lines:

> *And shake the yoke of inauspicious stars*
> *From this world-weary flesh.*

I would remember Anne Hathaway as I remembered that mature woman who taught me the ways of love in an apartment in Lübeck so many years ago. (I tried to recall that woman, but I could only recover the wallpaper, which was yellow, and the light that streamed in through the window. This first failure might have foreshadowed those to come.)

I had hypothesized that the images of that wondrous memory would be primarily visual. Such was not the case. Days later, as I was shaving, I spoke into the mirror a string of words that puzzled me; a colleague informed me that they were from Chaucer's 'A. B. C.' One afternoon, as I was leaving the British Museum, I began whistling a very simple melody that I had never heard before.

The reader will surely have noted the common thread that links these first revelations of the memory: it was, in spite of the splendor of some metaphors, a good deal more auditory than visual.

De Quincey says that our brain is a palimpsest. Every new text covers the previous one, and is in turn covered by the text that follows – but all-powerful Memory is able to exhume any impression, no matter how momentary it might have been, if given sufficient stimulus. To judge by the will he left, there had been not a single book in Shakespeare's house, not even the Bible, and yet everyone is familiar with the books he so often repaired to: Chaucer, Gower, Spenser, Christopher Marlowe, Holinshed's *Chronicle,* Florio's Montaigne, North's Plutarch. I possessed, at least potentially, the memory that had been Shakespeare's; the reading (which is to say the rereading) of those old volumes would, then, be the stimulus I sought. I also reread the sonnets, which are his work of greatest immediacy. Once in a while I came up with the explication, or with many explications. Good lines demand to be read aloud; after a few days I effortlessly recovered the harsh *r*'s and open vowels of the sixteenth century.

In an article I published in the *Zeitschrift für germanische Philologie,* I wrote that Sonnet 127 referred to the memorable defeat of the Spanish Armada. I had forgotten that Samuel Butler had advanced that same thesis in 1899.

A visit to Stratford-on-Avon was, predictably enough, sterile.

Then came the gradual transformation of my dreams. I was to be granted neither splendid nightmares *à la* de Quincey nor pious allegorical visions in the manner of his master Jean Paul; it was unknown rooms and faces that entered my nights. The first face I identified was Chapman's; later there was Ben Jonson's, and the face of one of the poet's neighbors, a person who does not figure in the biographies but whom Shakespeare often saw.

The man who acquires an encyclopedia does not thereby acquire every line, every paragraph, every page, and every illustration; he acquires the *possibility* of becoming familiar with one and another of those things. If that is the case with a concrete, and relatively simple, entity (given, I mean, the alphabetical order of its parts, etc.), then what must happen with a thing which is abstract and variable – *ondoyant et divers?* A dead man's magical memory, for example?

No one may capture in a single instant the fullness of his entire past. That gift was never granted even to Shakespeare, so far as I know, much less to me, who was but his partial heir. A man's memory is not a summation; it is a chaos of vague possibilities. St Augustine speaks, if I am not mistaken, of the palaces and the caverns of memory. That second metaphor is the more fitting one. It was into those caverns that I descended.

Like our own, Shakespeare's memory included regions, broad regions, of shadow – regions that he willfully rejected. It was not without shock that I remembered how Ben Jonson had made him recite Latin and Greek hexameters, and how his ear – the incomparable ear of Shakespeare – would go astray in many of them, to the hilarity of his fellows.

I knew states of happiness and darkness that transcend common human experience.

Without my realizing it, long and studious solitude had prepared me for the docile reception of the miracle. After some thirty days, the dead man's memory had come to animate me fully. For one curiously happy week, I almost believed myself Shakespeare. His work renewed itself for me. I know that for Shakespeare the moon was less the moon than it was Diana, and less Diana than that dark drawn-out word *moon*. I noted another discovery: Shakespeare's apparent instances of inadvertence – those *absences dans l'infini* of which Hugo apologetically speaks – were deliberate. Shakespeare tolerated them – or actually interpolated them – so that his discourse, destined for the stage, might appear to be spontaneous, and not overly polished and artificial *(nicht allzu glatt und gekünstelt)*. That same goal inspired him to mix his metaphors:

> *my way of life*
> *Is fall'n into the sear, the yellow leaf.*

One morning I perceived a sense of guilt deep within his memory. I did not try to define it; Shakespeare himself has done so for all time. Suffice it to say that the offense had nothing in common with perversion.

I realized that the three faculties of the human soul – memory, understanding, and will – are not some mere Scholastic fiction. Shakespeare's memory was able to reveal to me only the circumstances of *the man* Shakespeare. Clearly, these circumstances do not constitute the uniqueness of *the poet*; what matters is the literature the poet produced with that frail material.

I was naive enough to have contemplated a biography, just as Thorpe had. I soon discovered, however, that that literary genre requires a talent for writing that I do not possess. I do not know how to tell a story. I do not know how to tell *my own* story, which is a great deal more extraordinary than Shakespeare's. Besides, such a book would be pointless. Chance, or fate, dealt Shakespeare those trivial terrible things that all men know; it was his gift to be able to transmute them into fables, into characters that were much more alive than the gray man who dreamed them, into verses which will never be abandoned, into verbal music. What purpose would it serve to unravel that wondrous fabric, besiege and mine the tower, reduce to the modest proportions of a documentary biography or a realistic novel the sound and fury of *Macbeth*?

Goethe, as we all know, is Germany's official religion; the worship of Shakespeare, which we profess not without nostalgia, is more private. (In England, the official religion is Shakespeare, who is so unlike the English; England's sacred book, however, is the Bible.)

Throughout the first stage of this adventure I felt the joy of being Shakespeare; throughout the last, terror and oppression. At first the waters of the two memories did not mix; in time, the great torrent of Shakespeare threatened to flood my own modest stream – and very nearly did so. I noted with some nervousness that I was gradually forgetting the language of my parents. Since personal identity is based on memory, I feared for my sanity.

My friends would visit me; I was astonished that they could not see that I was in hell.

I began not to understand the everyday world around me *(die alltägliche Umwelt)*. One morning I became lost in a welter of great shapes forged in iron, wood, and glass. Shrieks and deafening noises assailed and confused me. It took me some time (it seemed an infinity) to recognize the engines and cars of the Bremen railway station.

As the years pass, every man is forced to bear the growing burden of his memory. I staggered beneath two (which sometimes mingled) – my own and the incommunicable other's.

The wish of all things, Spinoza says, is to continue to be what they are. The stone wishes to be stone, the tiger, tiger – and I wanted to be Hermann Sörgel again.

I have forgotten the date on which I decided to free myself. I hit upon the easiest way: I dialed telephone numbers at random. The voice of a child or a woman would answer; I believed it was my duty to respect their vulnerable estates. At last a man's refined voice answered.

'Do you,' I asked, 'want Shakespeare's memory? Consider well: it is a solemn thing I offer, as I can attest.'

An incredulous voice replied:

'I will take that risk. I accept Shakespeare's memory.'

I explained the conditions of the gift. Paradoxically, I felt both a *nostalgie* for the book I should have written, and now never would, and a fear that the guest, the specter, would never abandon me.

I hung up the receiver and repeated, like a wish, these resigned words:

Simply the thing I am shall make me live.

I had invented exercises to awaken the antique memory; I had now to seek others to erase it. One of many was the study of the mythology of William Blake, that rebellious disciple of Swedenborg. I found it to be less complex than merely complicated.

That and other paths were futile; all led me to Shakespeare.

I hit at last upon the only solution that gave hope courage: strict, vast music – Bach.

P.S. (1924) – I am now a man among men. In my waking hours I am Professor Emeritus Hermann Sörgel; I putter about the card catalog and compose erudite trivialities, but at dawn I sometimes know that the person dreaming is that other man. Every so often in the evening I am unsettled by small, fleeting memories that are perhaps authentic.

Guy de Maupassant · *Moonlight* · 9780241619803

Carson McCullers · *The Ballad of the Sad Café* · 9780241590546

Yukio Mishima · *Death in Midsummer* · 9780241630853

Vladimir Nabokov · *Nabokov's Dozen* · 9780241630884

Anaïs Nin · *A Spy in the House of Love* · 9780241614686

George Orwell · *Shooting an Elephant* · 9780241630099

Dorothy Parker · *Big Blonde* · 9780241609934

Edgar Allan Poe · *The Masque of the Red Death* · 9780241573754

Alexander Pushkin · *The Queen of Spades* · 9780241573761

Rainer Maria Rilke · *Letters to a Young Poet* · 9780241620038

Françoise Sagan · *Bonjour Tristesse* · 9780241630891

Saki · *Reginald's Christmas Revel* · 9780241597026

Arthur Schnitzler · *Dream Story* · 9780241620229

Sam Selvon · *Calypso in London* · 9780241630877

Georges Simenon · *My Friend Maigret* · 9780241630792

John Steinbeck · *Of Mice and Men* · 9780241620236

Leo Tolstoy · *The Cossacks* · 9780241573778

Yuko Tsushima · *Territory of Light* · 9780241620243

Sylvia Townsend Warner · *Lolly Willowes* · 9780241573785

Edith Wharton · *Summer* · 9780241630815

Oscar Wilde · *The Star-Child* · 9780241597033

Virginia Woolf · *Street Haunting* · 9780241677100

Stefan Zweig · *Chess* · 9780241630822

For rights reasons, not all titles available in the USA and Canada.